# LADY! THIS IS LOVE!

Dallas Day has finally qualified as a nurse and a marvellous opportunity arises to work at Miss Vaughan's prestigious nursing home. Dallas yearns for love and believes she has found it on meeting Dr Harper, the expert surgeon with the Valentino looks. But to her surprise his wife turns up as a patient and Dallas is given the task of looking after her. This gives Dallas more time to see Dr Harper but he is still unobtainable, despite his failing marriage. Dallas's heartache and confusion lead her to seek a new life, free of the traumas of love, in Malta.

# LADY! THIS IS LOVE!

URSULA BLOOM

as Sheila Burns

*A Lythway Book*

CHIVERS PRESS
BATH

First published 1938
by
Cassell & Company Ltd
This Large Print edition published by
Chivers Press
by arrangement with
the author's estate
1990

ISBN 0 7451 1050 9

**British Library Cataloguing in Publication Data**

Bloom, Ursula, *1895–1984*
Lady! This is love!—(A Lythway book).
I. Title
823′.912 [F]

ISBN 0–7451–1050–9

TO
PHYLLIS MANNIN

# CONTENTS

# LADY! THIS IS LOVE!

## CHAPTER ONE

# I INTRODUCE MYSELF

I suppose that we all think our own story is the most interesting in all the world, and really I dare say it is of very little interest to those people outside your own circle. And yet I wonder? For all this I have a burning desire to write about what happened to me, because I feel that it has been different. It has been absorbing, and I believe that it will hold you because it is *true*.

I am a nurse.

I trained in a big London hospital, under the vigilance of one of the strictest Sisters to be found. I worked early and late, until I thought that my feet would drop right off me as I stood. I very soon gave up the idea that a nurse's life consisted of patting pillows and saying 'There now!' in a tenderly sympathetic voice, and I resigned myself to scrubbing and to scouring and to wishing that I had never attempted the job. But I went on. I went on because I knew my people would laugh if I cut it all and went home. I knew that they would say I was spineless, and I wasn't going to stand for that.

There were days when I got dog-tired. Night duty when I spent the live-long night on my feet. Breakfast at eight, then attending lectures when your head is nodding and your eyes closing for the want of sleep. But let the powers-that-be catch you nodding, and it means dismissal!

I knew that.

Well, we have all been through it.

Three solid years, three hard, and almost defeating, years, with a stiff exam. at the end which sets you quaking. Then suddenly a day when I was called up before the Matron (a most frightening old lady) with a certificate in my hand which read 'Fully Qualified.'

I had done my time.

I was a fully-fledged nurse.

After all this, maybe you wonder what I am like? Well, I'm ordinary, I have brown eyes and brown hair, which I long to go blonde, but which never will; I have a pale complexion and too red a mouth. The very alarming Sister swore that I used lip-stick, but that is not true. That would have meant dismissal all right, because as a nurse there are very few things that you may do in that way. I'm not too tall. I'm the sort of nurse who flits up and down a ward, and who goes on and on slaving all her life. I didn't suppose that I would marry. In my job you don't get an awful lot of chances, and it wasn't as if I had people of my own who could give me a good time off duty.

Mother died when I was a child and Father is

very old, and rather a remote sort of a person. He lives with my married sister, and my married sister is one of those people who, had I failed in my training, would have said, 'There, I knew you couldn't stick it!'

I've had to put up with a lot from Alice, but then lots of us have sisters like that and don't make a song about it.

I am called Dallas Day, and I work from seven-thirty in the morning until seven-thirty at night; then I am generally so tired that I flop on to the bed. I have not much time to enjoy myself. I haven't time to meet people. No time for anything that really matters in one's personal and intimate life.

I love my work.

Please don't think that I am complaining. I always wanted to be a nurse from the time when I bound and bandaged my dolls in the old garden at home. What is more, I would be a nurse if I had my time again, but it *is* a hard life.

I suppose in every girl's existence there must be the longing for marriage and motherhood. There is the yearning for romance. It is a latent instinct that you cannot choke down in you, leastways I couldn't; I've tried, but it won't go.

Love was something which I always thought would never come to me just because I would never get the chance to meet the man of my dreams. Yet for all this the chance came. That is why I am writing this now.

It seemed that suddenly a fairy stepped into my life, and drew back the curtain of possibility and said, 'Lady, this is love!'

That is why I am taking up my pen now, to tell you the story which is my own; the story that nobody else knows but me.

## 2

When I had finished training, for a short time I wandered restlessly through most of the different phases of private nursing. Then suddenly I happened to get offered a post in Miss Vaughan's nursing home.

I was tremendously lucky in this, because hers is in a very enviable position. The home stands in one of the great, quiet streets of London which lie round Harley Street. I liked Miss Vaughan. She was a woman of infinite understanding, with calm grey eyes that looked you through and through, and grey hair which had never been cut short.

She was one of the few nurses who had not become an automaton through over-training; she was still a woman. She had kept her own soul.

Because I liked her so much I took the job when it was offered to me, and came here to live in her home. What is more, I knew that I was enormously lucky. The staff was largely composed of older nurses, who had been with her for many years and who all worked together like the cog-wheels of some giant machine. The rooms were luxurious. Stepping inside the building, you would never have thought that you were going into a nursing home, but into some lovely private house. Quiet carpets, exquisite flowers, and suddenly through a half-open door the glimpse of a room decorated beautifully (she had a special colour scheme for every room), and further flowers. She believed in minds mending bodies, and for that reason she said it was important that sick people should lie in lovely surroundings, and I am quite sure that she was right.

They put me on to the theatre work.

The newest and junior nurses always get all the rotten jobs that are going; that is one of the laws of hospital work, so that I rather expected I should get something of this kind. Naturally I like to have a patient of my own, and all the responsibility of caring for that patient. I like to get someone ready for the theatre and, receiving them back from the surgeon's hands, nurse them into health again.

But directly I got to Miss Vaughan's she called me into her little private room and said, 'Nurse Day, your first duty will be in the theatre'; then I knew that I should probably be there for some time.

It was, of course, experience, for all the most eminent surgeons in London went to operate at

Miss Vaughan's, and people who were just names before were working in the deathly stillness of that theatre, a stillness only broken by the ripple of anæsthetic passing through tubes, by the word of command, or the rustle of a starched skirt as Sister obeyed that command.

I can see Sister Bridges now. She was old and white-haired, with blue eyes bent on the surgeon, but her heart was in her work. They just lived for their work in that home; they had given the best of their lives to it, and existed for nothing else. You couldn't expect it of them.

I made friends with the only other young nurse in the building, Nurse Tennyson, called Tenny for short. Tenny was a bit wild, I must say, and she made great fun (sometimes not too kind fun) of the 'old fossils,' as she called the other nurses. She had been born in Scotland, and she had come to the home because she thought that it would afford chances to meet people, only somehow she had been kept so busy that none of the anticipated chances had come her way.

'I always hope that I'll meet some rich patient who wants a permanent nurse, and offers marriage to me,' she would say with a twinkle in her eye.

Poor Tenny! I liked her, though I always did feel that one day there would be a dreadful rumpus with her, but all the same she had been in the home four years, so she could not have been as gay as she sounded.

She mentioned Dr. Harper to me. All along I had an idea that his name was a pass-word to the home. They doted on him.

'He is marvellous,' she told me; 'he just won't let his patients die. You should see that man in the theatre; he is worth watching. He is a miracle.'

I wished she would not talk about him that way, but what she said intrigued me. Most doctors are casual in a theatre, almost rude. There is no time for courtesy, and the idea that romances occur there is a very mistaken one. But the impression she made on me about Dr. Harper stayed, so that when I did see him I was already interested. I was already intrigued. I was busy with the sterilizer when he came in. He was younger than most of our surgeons; tall and dark, with eyes that were quickly alert, and a mouth that was tender and affectionate. You could not look at that mouth without realizing that it might mean everything in the world to you. It sounds silly. It sounds as though I was a love-sick young girl, ready to fall in love; in point of fact I was nothing of the kind.

I watched him coming into the theatre fastening the mask over his face, and after that I could only see his eyes; all the time I knew that they were the eyes of a fighting man. He did not mean to lose to death, whatever happened. He had an extraordinary personality; I felt that;

what is more, I am sure that I should have felt it if Tenny hadn't told me of it beforehand. I had the strange, rather uncanny feeling that he was going to mean something to me, yet all the time I knew that he couldn't mean anything to me; it was just stupid of me. I pulled myself together with a jerk.

The patient was under when she was wheeled in. It was a tricky case. I personally should have said that she did not stand one chance in a hundred, but I knew that Dr. Harper was not feeling the same way about it. I had nothing to do but stand back and watch, and, as I stood there, I realized the extraordinary will-power of this man. He was the most determined personality that I have ever met as he bent over her.

From the head of the table the anæsthetist whispered a warning. 'The heart is bad. She won't stick much more.'

I saw Sister Bridges' eyes above her mask, and they were distressed. She was one of those people who panic, yet who only show it in their eyes. But the doctor did not turn a hair. He worked on like an automaton, those clever fingers touching this and that, deftly and without hesitation. He went on operating without wasting a second.

'She has *got* to stick it,' he said between his teeth; 'what's more, she has *got* to live.'

I felt then that he was one of those men who

could make you do anything that he wanted. I felt that he would never relinquish his hold on a patient's life if he could possibly help it. He went on, and in the next few minutes I saw him perform what was nothing less than a miracle; it was something that I am quite sure no other man could have done.

Afterwards, when they rushed her back to her room, I stood by the basin offering him a towel as he washed. Suddenly he seemed to relax. He whipped off mask and cap, and I saw that his brow was wet with perspiration, and that the dark hair clung to it. Those eyes which had been so determined and so full of that fighting spirit looked at me in a surprised way, as though he noticed me for the first time.

'You're new here?'

'Yes, sir, I am new.' And I felt like a little girl at school—a little girl meeting a fresh teacher for the first time. It may sound absurd, but I couldn't look at him. I couldn't look him between the eyes.

He said, 'They need some new blood; there are far too many of the old school, and it doesn't help temperamental patients. It is a good thing to have someone fresh. Where were you trained?'

I told him, and it seemed to me that he looked me through; all the while I felt gauche and nervous before him. I felt as though something trembled inside me, and that he could read my thoughts, which made it all the worse, for I knew that I wanted to make a good impression on him, yet here I was blushing like a schoolgirl.

He finished wiping his hands and flung the towel aside. I should have been angry with most doctors who did that, but you couldn't be angry with him. He was dog-tired from the operation, and I don't wonder. He had exhausted much of his own vitality in working for the life of the woman. And he *had* saved her life. He had operated marvellously.

He said, 'I hope you'll be on on the next op. Are you theatre nurse?'

And I said 'Yes, sir,' but I don't think he stopped to listen to my answer, for he seemed to be thinking about something else.

Then he rushed off.

## 3

I told Tenny about it when she came into the sterilizing room, where I was finishing up.

'I felt such a fool,' I explained.

'Oh, he makes you feel like that,' said she; 'he is so awfully good-looking and so fascinating. He ought not to be a doctor. He ought to have been a Rudolf Valentino—I always think he looks awfully like Valentino, don't you? The odd thing is that he hasn't any time for women and he makes that pretty plain before you know him very long. He doesn't like them.'

'He seemed kind enough,' I said.

'Oh, yes, just kind enough, but nothing more. You'll never get any further with Ray Harper, my girl, so don't you fancy it.'

'I'm not fancying it.'

A bell began to ring.

'That's little Mrs. Twenty-Four. Sometimes I feel that she rings that bell to spite me. The moment I have got a cup of tea, bang goes that bell. Half a moment,' and off she went.

I sat there in the sterilizing room, still thinking about what she had said. I suppose it is because I am plain and rather simple that I never had expected to be attracted to any man, yet somehow this had suddenly happened to me. Ray Harper was somebody you went on thinking about. The way he looked at you, and those calm, almost dreadfully calm hands of his. I knew that I should never forget his fight for that woman's life this afternoon, and undoubtedly he had saved her. It wasn't as though I hadn't seen big men operate before; I had, but I have never seen anything so clever as the operation he had performed this afternoon.

But it was all stupid of me.

Quite early on in my training, when hordes of medical students were going round the wards, I had been warned by the Sister who lectured to us.

'Never set your cap at a doctor, nurses; it

doesn't come off. Never think of a doctor as being anything but a machine, and think of yourselves as being part of the machine which helps him accomplish his task.'

Somehow I could not think of Ray Harper as being only a machine.

'You'll get over it,' said Tenny, coming back cheerfully; 'you'll find that when he snubs you you feel awful, but you'll pull yourself together.'

'It isn't anything like that.'

'Isn't it? With most new nurses it is. But they all learn in time,' and she laughed about it.

Just at first at the home I had so much work to do that I couldn't think of him very often; at that time there seemed to be a large amount of emergency ops. rushed in, and we were working from all hours. When I did think of Ray Harper, I was a little ashamed, because it was schoolgirlish and silly, and I had no right to be schoolgirlish and silly with my training.

Then suddenly I found him in the theatre again. That grim personality which actually compelled a patient to live. That haste and precision, the way he instantly stayed bleeding (he was the cleanest surgeon who came to us) and the way he relaxed directly the operation was over.

He always had a smile for me.

He always said, 'Oh, hello, it's you,' when he sank back afterwards, with that tired look in his eyes, and those hands which had been so strong, and which suddenly seemed to have no life left in them.

'You take too much out of yourself,' I said one day; it was only about the third time I had seen him. 'You give too much of yourself.'

And he answered, 'My patients have a right to demand it of me, and I have no right to deny it to them. My job is to see them well again.'

Somehow then I saw that grimness, that bleak coldness which Tenny said he could put up between himself and any nurse who worried him. I did not talk of his personality again.

At twenty-six one had one's dreams.

Perhaps you will think that a quite plain nurse with no prospects at all ought not to have any dreams, but they were surging about one hero for me; and he was the hero. No one need ever know, I told myself, and looked upon it as being a precious secret which I could hold fast with myself.

But I was wrong.

Tenny suspected it.

'Never mind, you'll get over it,' she said. 'We have all felt that way about him at some time or other, but it isn't any good. He is wrapped up in his work. Nothing else ever happens for him, so don't you think it.'

'I'm not thinking it.'

She laughed at me and said, 'Oh, yes, you

are. Indulge the feeling for a while, it will fade.'

Only it didn't fade.

## 4

I had been at the home a couple of months, I suppose, and had worked hard as theatre nurse; I had watched him operate, and had seen patients come and go and had heard the nurses chatter, when one day Miss Vaughan sent for me herself.

She and I got on very well together on the whole; she was a demanding matron—she always wanted the best of her nurses, and nothing second best would do, but at the same time she was fair and just. A lot of the matrons in hospital are nothing of the sort, and I always have said that you can work where there is justice, even though it may be a carping justice.

Directly I saw her I knew that she was agitated, although she appeared to be outwardly so composed; but by this time I had got to know her fairly well and knew what lay behind her outward demeanour.

'An appendix case is being rushed in,' she said, 'and she is going to number eighteen.'

Number eighteen was one of our most expensive rooms, which meant that it must be an important person who could afford to pay an important sum of money.

'Her husband has telephoned to us, and he asks particularly that you should take charge of the case. She is highly strung and imaginative, and will need most tactful handling. Her husband is confident that you will look after her very well.'

Her husband! I had no idea who this might be, and racked my brain to think, but could not put a name to the patient. I would have asked, but Miss Vaughan had given us all a lecture only a few days previously, saying that names were matterless, and that individuality did not count in hospital; the great thing was to think of your patient as a case.

So far having done nothing but theatre work in the home, and being dead sick of sterilizers and swabs, the idea of having a case of my own was an enchanting one. I felt myself colouring.

'I will do all I can,' I promised, and then it struck me as being very peculiar that the husband (whom I could not possibly know) should have asked for me. I inquired, 'What is her name? It seems so queer that the husband should have asked for me.'

Outside, in the little corridor beyond the comfortable room which was Miss Vaughan's, I could hear the sound of a new arrival, and guessed that it was the patient who was coming in for her appendix.

Miss Vaughan drew herself up a little. She said, 'In nursing we all have to keep secrets. I don't suppose that anyone here knew that Dr. Harper was married. It is his wife, and I think by the sound of it she has just arrived.'

She got up and went to the door, and I followed her with my eyes, thankful that, for the time being, she seemed almost to have forgotten that I was here at all. I did not know what to think. I suppose until that moment I had not been so horribly sure of my own feelings, but then (when she said, 'I don't suppose that anyone here knew that Dr. Harper was married'), I realized the truth. This was not just a light, happy-go-lucky, quick-come, quick-go emotion, but something a great deal deeper.

It seemed dreadful to me at that particular moment that I could feel this way. Life is topsy-turvy. It is allowed that a man should fall in love, and if his affections are unrequited, then people only feel pity for him. But with a woman life is not so kind. I knew that I was just a silly girl who had committed what is the unforgivable sin for a nurse, fallen for the first good-looking doctor with whom I had worked. It was the very thing that I had so often condemned in others, yet here was I doing it myself. I wanted to think. I wanted to pull myself together, and I had a horrid idea that I wasn't going to get time. I wanted to tell Miss Vaughan that I would not work for Dr. Harper's wife, and that I hated the idea of nursing her.

I did not get the chance.

Miss Vaughan had hurried out into the hall,

and luckily my common sense and training came to my aid. I found myself, outwardly completely calm, hurrying after her. Directly I got outside I saw Mrs. Harper sitting there. She was drawn and white; her little face had faded under its mask of make-up so that the rouge looked clown-like under the sunken eyes, and merely emphasized the ghastly pallow of her skin.

She was obviously in great pain, and although she wore luxurious clothes, looked pathetic as she sank into a little heap. It was funny, but before I had seen her I had been deeply prejudiced against her. I can't think why. After all, Dr. Harper had every right to be married, just as she had every right to marry him; it was no business of mine. Then, seeing her, I suddenly realized that she was wretchedly ill, and I suppose all my nursing instincts came to my aid.

I went to her gently and took her arm.

'Come,' I said, 'I'll see after you; I am here to make you better.'

She turned and clung to me. She was very, very pretty. She had eyes which reminded me of violets, the kind that you find in country lanes at the beginning of April, very dark and dewy. She had a peevish little mouth, but an exquisite skin, and hair like silk. She had everything, this girl, beauty and charm, and the one man in the world. Yet something told me then that she wasn't happy.

I got her up to her room. It was the luxurious one with the soft, pale green silk cushions and eiderdown, and the creamy white walls. When she saw it she gave a little gasp. 'I oughtn't to have come here; green isn't lucky.'

I knew that we were absolutely full and that there wasn't another room to give her, and I knew that Dr. Harper liked our home and trusted Miss Vaughan, therefore he would not want to take his wife somewhere else.

'Oh, but green can be terribly lucky to some people,' I told her, 'and this is one of our brightest rooms. Nothing has ever gone wrong here yet. The best patients come here.'

She looked at me helplessly, and then sank down on the end of the bed and began to cry.

'I'll die. I know that I'll die.'

A nurse is used to difficult patients. I put an arm round her comfortingly, because I knew instinctively that she needed consolation. She was not one of those patients whom you can scold into doing what you want. Sympathy, and she would do whatever you asked her. 'Come now,' I said, 'you mustn't get that idea into your head. People don't die with appendixes, you know. Not nowadays. I'm here to see you through it and to make quite sure that you get well and strong again.'

And all the while I was trying to forget that she was his wife. I was trying to tell myself that

I was behaving like a silly schoolgirl myself. He was a doctor whose work I had watched and admired, a man whose personality had made itself felt in the theatre and who was undoubtedly brilliantly clever. Beyond that I ought not to think. Yet I did think. I wish people could help their thoughts; I wish so much that I could be prosaic, and calm, and realize that the first duty of a nurse is to be an automaton, and that dreams, of the kind that I was dreaming, were not for people like myself.

I helped her out of her things.

I realized then that she was extravagant for everything was of sheer silk, stockings like gossamer, and absurd little satin shoes. She shivered, poor little soul, and I felt sorry for her. I wouldn't like to be on the verge of an operation myself. I tucked her into bed with a hot water-bottle in case the pain came on again, and I tried to allay her fears as best I could .

'You won't know anything about it,' I said. 'You'll just wake up to find that it is all over, and that the pain has gone away and you only feel a bit weak.'

'The pain was awful when it came on,' she confessed, 'and I am not awfully good at bearing it.'

She began to cry again.

'You shan't have to bear any more,' I promised her.

When I had got her a little quieter I

unpacked her bag for her. It was a crocodile dressing-case containing a tortoiseshell dressing set with her monogram in brilliants on it, and I guessed this had been his wedding gift to her. It hurt me that she could have so much wherewith to add to her attractions, for everything about her was exquisite. There were nighties made of satin, and wisps of dressing-jackets. I thought, 'No wonder she attracted him when she was so lovely, and he could afford all this extra beatuy.' It did not seem to be fair to think that one woman could have so much.

Then he came into the room.

A doctor on duty and a doctor off duty are two very different men. I was to realize that.

'You'll let me see Flower?' he asked, and then with a smile, 'I asked for you. I knew you wouldn't be a dragon and you'd be sweet to her.'

What could I say?

I hoped that my eyes did not give me away as I stood aside for him to go to her bed, and stand there gazing down at her. There are some things in life that hurt too much to bear; that was why I slipped out of the door and into the corridor beyond. I had got a lump in my throat. I was still thinking it seemed so hard that Flower Harper should have so much and I so little. All the time I knew that I was wrong.

# 5

Outside I met Tenny.

She turned an amazed and gaping face to me. 'They say it is *his wife*? Surely it can't be? And he has asked for *you* to nurse her?'

'Hush!' and I tried again to be calm and collected so that Tenny should not guess how much she was worrying me. 'She is his wife. Miss Vaughan said that very few people knew about it; I don't know why I took it on, but apparently he did ask for me.'

'My goodness! I should think very few people did know about it! Nobody knew. Nobody guessed. We all thought that he was a handsome bachelor. What a bombshell to drop on to us!'

At that particular moment I knew that I was on the verge of breaking down, and whatever happened I must not do it. I had got to stick this somehow.

I said, 'This ought to be enough to convince you that all your teasing was just nonsense. She is terribly pretty, and I think when she has got over the op. she will be rather amusing.'

Outside the porter was bringing up flowers. There was a great basket of mimosa, hyper-sweet, and a little note attached to the golden basket full of golden flowers.

The little note said: *Love from Bill.*

The porter carried also a sheaf of lilies, a bunch which must have cost a young fortune, and, becoming used as I was to seeing expensive flowers, I just stood and stared at these.

'Yes, they're good, aren't they?' said the porter. 'It was Dr. Harper who brought these in for her. Fancy him being married! We all thought that he was a bachelor gentleman.'

I took the flowers in. I don't know why, but I did feel then that some people got all the fun, and all the luck. I'd have to go on working hard all my life, and never have anybody to send me flowers like this. If I got ill I should be pushed away into a corner to get over it with scant sympathy and very little understanding. And I'd never have anybody to love me. Perhaps that hurt most of all. This girl seemed to have so much, too much for one person. Then I told myself not to be unreasonable. Each of us has a different chance in life, each has a different destiny, and it isn't much good complaining. Flower Harper had been born with what you would call a silver spoon in her mouth, and mine was nothing of the sort.

I went into the room.

The doctor was leaning over her tenderly. He had laid his hands on either side of her face, and was speaking in a low voice; somehow the sight of him like that, looking at her so wistfully, speaking so kindly, hurt me more than I liked to think. I mustn't be a fool, I told myself. I must treat it all as part of the day's march.

'Some flowers for you,' I said, and tried hard

to asume that bright 'nurse's' voice.

I set them down beside her. That was when he called me to him. He came across the room with me, to the passage outside. He said, 'You'll take care of her, won't you?' and I realized that he was desperately nervous. 'She's frail, she isn't strong. She is more highly strung than most people, and therefore she feels things more. You'll be good to her?'

'There isn't any need for anxiety.' I found myself talking to him as one always talks to all anxious relatives. It seemed queer that, although he knew so much about surgery, that knowledge was not helping him now. He was nervous as a kitten.

'Yes, of course you'll see after her, and of course she'll be all right,' he pulled himself together, and smiled at me. There was something quite childlike about that smile. 'Funny that I should get this way, isn't it? It is all so different when it is a person you love.'

I left him because I knew that I was not the one to comfort him, and the most distressing part is that there is so little that you can do to comfort anyone like that. Facing an operation for a relative is so very different from facing one in the theatre when it is no relation, and you are not personally affected by it.

'She'll want me,' I said.

As I went back into the room, I told myself, 'I've got to treat her impersonally. I've got to forget that she is his wife, and that is the only way I shall be able to worry through.'

## 6

She was lying there fingering the mimosa which stretched out from the golden basket. She turned her head to me weakly. 'Oh, I'll be so thankful when all this is over,' she said.

'Yes, of course you will. It won't be half so bad as you think,' I promised her.

'From Bill.' She had the card in her hand, and was turning it over and over. 'Nurse, can you keep a secret?'

'I have to keep a good many in my job.'

'I've got a tiny note that I have scribbled. When I have gone down to the theatre will you get it posted for me?' She began to cry a little, they were the usual tears of self-pity which are so natural in anybody before an operation. 'Don't tell anybody, specially Ray. He must never know.'

I promised, of course, and it was a promise that I meant to keep, but I was dreadfully worried by it. I connected the two, 'Love from Bill,' and 'Don't tell anybody, specially Ray,' and somehow I distrusted her. I knew then that there was something underhand going on, something which I hated to think about, because she had the best husband in the world. He was one of those men who would do anything for her, kindness itself, I knew, and he must be desperately in love with her.

He was one of those men that any woman would have wanted, with that whimsical yet tender mouth, and those eyes which looked right down into your soul. I knew that I should never forget the first time that I saw him, when he was fighting for that woman's life in the operating theatre; I knew that then he had made an impression on me which I should never lose. I couldn't help it, I should always be attracted to him whatever anybody else said, and even though it might be wrong, it was something that I should never be able to choke down entirely.

I got her ready for the theatre. I gave her the first dose of that merciful and kind anæsthetic which sends people to sleep in their own beds, so that they know nothing of the theatre itself, or of going down to it, or of the coming back again. When she was dead off, they came for her, and wheeled her away, a limp, white little figure, pathetically small.

I turned to, and got the room ready for her return. There were things to be put straight, the bed to be warmed, and everything made comfortable so that she should be as happy as possible.

Whilst I was doing this I heard the door open behind me, and, thinking it was Tenny come in to give me a hand, called, 'You *would* come when I am almost through.' Too late, I saw that

I had made a most dreadful mistake. It was Ray Harper.

He laughed. 'You weren't expecting me?'

'Oh no, I thought it was one of the other nurses,' and I was ashamed that I had turned crimson.

He came to the foot of the empty bed which was waiting for her, and stood there watching. He said: 'She is going to be all right, isn't she? She *is* going to be all right?' and I saw that in this afternoon he had aged, and that his face was white and drawn.

I did not know what to do.

Behind him stood the trolley, white-covered with the dressings, and the medicines all shrouded and ghost-like, before him the empty white bed waiting for Flower to be laid back in it. The room was stripped of flowers, it was gaunt and bare, and in it I could only see his eyes tormented by doubt, the eyes of a man who had forgotten his medicine in his love for his wife.

'Appendicitis is not dangerous when caught in such an early stage,' I said.

He nodded. 'I'm being a fool, aren't I? They always say that a doctor makes the biggest fuss!'

'It is only natural. You see dangers ahead for your own which you would never think of for a stranger.'

'It does worry me.' Then he jerked himself together. 'I'm glad you are seeing after her; I asked particularly for you. Flower isn't an easy person to nurse, it has made all the difference in the world, knowing that you have her in your charge. You won't leave her, will you?'

When he looked at me like that, I could not say no, and yet I would have given everything that I had if I might have refused to take on the case. Flower had so much in comparison with myself; she could look so lovely, while I am a plain woman and in my hard little cotton uniform had nothing wherewith to make myself look better. I suppose that I was jealous.

More and more flowers kept arriving for her, and I made the excuse to see after them, yet all the while I knew that he was pacing that bedroom, and realized that he dare not have gone to the theatre with her, and was feeling too sick with anxiety to be anything but restless.

I heard the lift coming up with the stretcher in it, and I went to meet it. They wheeled her out of the lift, and I knew by her colour that she had done well. The theatre Sister was at her side.

'Simple appendix,' she said briskly in answer to my inquiry, 'she'll be as right as rain in a fortnight,' and she stepped out towards the room which was ready.

I saw the doctor standing there. I don't believe that he saw either of us, but only his wife's face, and he knew also that she was doing well. Instantly his eyes lit up, the anxiety fell from him like a cloak, and he stood there watching us lift her on to the bed without a hint of dread which had been so obvious in him a few minutes before.

They had done the op. in record time.

'She's grand,' said the theatre Sister.

'She looks fine.'

She came round beautifully. When she had come to, she made a most terrible fuss, but then I had rather anticipated that she might. Her husband stood on one side of her, trying to stop her tears, but she insisted on crying her heart out from sheer self-pity. He was dreadfully distressed, and it worried me seeing him helpless to do anything for her, yet sitting there looking so anxious.

'She'll be better with strangers,' I told him, 'leave her to me, I'll manage her.'

'It seems like deserting her.'

'It is better for her. You'd say that in any other patient. She will pull herself together and be a different woman.'

He saw the logic of that, and in the doorway he put out a hand and wrung mine.

'You're a brick,' he said; 'if ever a woman was cut out to be a nurse, you are the one; and I knew then that he looked upon me purely as a piece of machinery and had never thought of me as being a woman at all.

Very soon after he had gone, she quietened down, and lay there, no longer crying and complaining, but watching me in a dazed, dozey sort of way. She wanted to know if I had posted the letter. She wanted the golden basket of mimosa brought much closer, so that she could see it better, and the beautiful lilies that her husband had sent her moved right away.

Then she fell into a deep sleep, and I left her in the hands of the night nurse when she was like that.

'HIS wife?' said the night nurse.

'Yes. I don't see why it seems so queer that he should be married.'

'It seems extraordinary to me. Nobody knew. How long has it been going on?'

It wasn't any business of ours, and I said so. I took a last look at her and left her for the night. In the morning she would be much better.

An appendix takes forty-eight hours of hard nursing; then you are generally through the wood. During those forty-eight hours, if I were away from her side, Mrs. Harper rang the bell. She wanted every moment of me, she wanted every ounce of my strength. There was something about her which seemed to sap my vitality, something which sucked the life from me.

'She'll make you quite ill,' Tenny said. 'I'd let her get on with her old appendix, and stew in her own juice. There is nothing much the matter with her, and what there is, is mostly put on.'

Which I had to admit was true.

As a nurse you see the inside life of patients, and I had known from the first that Flower Harper was spoilt. There came lovely gifts for her, a tiny dressing-jacket made entirely of swansdown, a little make-up outfit to slip under her pillow; all the newest books, boxes of chocolates of a size and shape that I had never seen before. Enormous chocolates, and she too frightened for her figure to be tempted by any one of them.

Appearance meant everything to her; appearance and Bill.

She got a little better and then she told me all manner of things about her husband. I didn't want to listen. But what could I do? I could not tell her that I respected and cared for him myself, perhaps too deeply, and that he meant everything to me. I had to sit there and listen, and these revelations were torture to me.

She told me about their marriage.

She had been touring with a seaside company during the summer, and Ray had sat in the stalls and had been attracted by her. They had got to know one another, and she, seeing that he was fascinated by her, had faked an illness and had been left behind when the company toured on.

It is extraordinary how even the trained brain can become blind when a man falls in love. He had never realized that her illness was a fake; he had fallen head over heels in love, and had not known that all the while she had gone out of her way to discover that he was rich.

'I dare say you think it is awful to marry a man for his money,' she said, 'but it is far more awful to be poor. I know, because I've had some. But Ray is so deadly serious. He has such idiotic ideas of living life seriously—and soberly. He sticks to that rotten old profession of his, and he does not like me doing things, and being happy. I always say that he ought to have been a Scotch Minister, and not a doctor at all. Oh, I've been through Hell with him.'

I was quite sure that this was not true, and thought it highly probable that he might have been through Hell with her. Yet he had never complained.

I said, 'Marriage means give and take, of course.'

And she turned from me impatiently.

She said, 'I believe you are a prude,' and once, 'You ought to have married Ray yourself, then you'd know what he is like. Smug! That's what he is!'

'Spoiling' was what I thought sounded to be much more like it.

## 7

On the fourth day she wanted new nighties. She had come into the home with the loveliest trousseau that I had ever seen, but there were not enough for her. Satin beauté with fine lace, patterned chiffon, georgette. Ray did not grumble. He sent in a dozen that afternoon, and I felt that they ought to have been tea-gowns, not nightdresses at all, but even they did not satisfy her.

'They're dowdy,' she said, and made a grimace, 'they are the sort of things that he *would* buy. You have some of them,' and she flung me across half a dozen ungraciously.

I wanted to say no, because they were quite unsuitable for me, and quite the loveliest that I had ever seen, but then I remembered that he had bought them. I suppose it ought not to have made any difference, and I must have been mad to think of such a thing, but human nature is queer, and it acts queerly and on impulses. I thanked her profusely, and she said in a disgruntled manner:

'Nonsense, you've done me a kindness. If I had sent them all back, Ray would have been angry with me. As long as somebody keeps them he doesn't care. Take them and forget about it.'

That night I slept in chiffon, and I was ashamed that I dreamed of him, and in the morning told myself that I was acting like a little fool, and was old enough to know better.

But logic does not help when you fall in love. I had found that out.

# 8

It was hurting me far too much.

The part that was most difficult was that I was a jealous little idiot. I hated seeing him hanging over her bed, stroking her soft fair hair, and hearing him say sweet and endearing things.

'Thank God,' I told myself, 'that an appendix is a short illness, and I shall soon be rid of them both.'

Them both! It had come to that.

The other nurses were naturally all eyes and ears, because each of them had suffered a passion for Ray in her time, and they had been tremendously intrigued discovering that he was married. Off-time was harassed. We trooped down to the meals whereat Miss Vaughan presided. In the sitting-room, a prim, austere little room, where no sunshine ever penetrated and which although it was called 'Nurses' relaxation room' was anything but an invitation to relax, everybody chatted about it.

I had not realized that Ray Harper was such a pet in the home, nor that they thought so highly of him, and that every nurse cared for him.

'He is one of those men,' said Tenny in a confidential mood, 'haven't you noticed it, there *are* men like that? Valentino, George Raft sort of men. You see them and you fall for them. They are forbidding rather than fascinating, and give you the idea of always holding something back.'

That was perhaps the truest thing she ever said. Ray Harper was one of those men born to fascinate women.

Only Miss Vaughan held her peace about it. I think she had summed Flower up in her own mind, and knew the sort of girl that she was. I had kept quiet about Bill, who had sent in the basket of mimosa, and about the letter I had had to post, but I knew that Flower was wondering how she could get him to see her while she was in the home without setting other people talking.

I said that she couldn't. It would be madness. Every nurse was out to see what she could, and nobody can chatter more than they can. I was so afraid that the news might eventually reach her husband and hurt him.

'Oh, bother him,' said Flower, 'he must learn to fight his own battles.'

It was then that I thought of the man who had fought for his patients' lives on the operating table with such a relentless determination, and who would not let them go. I thought of him, hopelessly incapable of fighting this shadowy figure of Bill, and the extravagances and spoilt whims of his wife.

'It is so wrong,' I told myself.

But all the time I was telling myself that it would end. A fortnight would see her back in her own home and then I should not be distressed by her, and worried. Another patient would fill this bed, and we should be able to forget Flower Harper.

Only it didn't end like that!

On the eighth day I found Dr. Harper in the sterilizing room. I was off duty and had gone down, sent by one of the other nurses, to have a look as to how the swabs were sterilizing. I found him there.

'I'm trespassing, I know,' he said laughing, 'but I have been looking for you, Nurse, and I want to have a chat with you.'

Nurse. It sounds such an impersonal word, and I hate to hear it. Nurse is so remote. Nobody has ever called me Dallas for years.

'It's about Flower. I dare say you have realized that she has taken an immense fancy to you. It really rests with you that she has made such a quick recovery and I cannot tell you how grateful I am to you for it.'

He held out his hand and took mine. I felt a lump in my throat as though I wanted to cry, which was quite silly of me, for nothing was more natural than that he should be grateful and want to say so. I had done nothing but what was my duty for his wife, and I wanted to tell him that, but the words would not come.

Then suddenly he said something which startled me. 'I know your name is Day,' he anounced, 'what else is it?'

I was so surprised that I told him.

'It is Dallas. Dallas Day.'

Only a few minutes before I had been thinking what ages it was since anybody had called me Dallas. I was tired of being just Nurse. It is everybody's name, and I wanted to have my own name for a change.

'I am going to ask you a favour,' he said.

'I shall be pleased to do anything that I can for you.'

'You understand Flower, and at times she is a bit of a handful. I dare say you have found that out already?'

I had.

'After this she is to go away for a change, which it is imperative that she should have. I dare not go with her because, after all, I have other people who have greater need of me, yet I don't want her to go alone.'

I thought instantly of Bill, the man I had never seen, knowing quite well that Ray had no idea about Bill. I did not know what was coming next.

'I've seen Miss Vaughan,' he said, 'and she is agreeable, and I am wondering if you would take Flower away for me?'

I shan't forget that moment.

All along I had been telling myself that the tension could not last, and that when she had gone I should be rid of them both and have time to re-establish my own feelings and to forget that I had ever thought foolishly of Ray Harper.

Because it was foolish. Anyway, just as a specialist and myself as an ordinary little nurse it had been too ridiculous, but when I knew that he was a married man then of course it was madness.

We stood there in the sterilizing room, burningly hot, for the sterilizer was going (they were operating within the hour), and Ray was standing there staring at me with beseeching eyes.

Charge of Flower!

To go away with her, reminded all the time that she was his wife. I felt then that nothing in the whole world could be more hateful. I wanted to scream: 'No, no, I CAN'T,' but then at the very moment when I was just going to tell him that it was quite impossible, another thought struck me.

If she left the home without me, then although I might have time to make myself sensible, I should so seldom see him. If I went away with her, I should meet him in his home-life, I should be seeing him for week-ends. It would be bad for me; it would hurt me, but it meant so much to me that I couldn't say no.

'You will do this for me, Dallas?' he asked.

For a moment I stood there quite still.

He did not know that I would do anything in the world for him. When he looked at me like that, compellingly and possessively, he must have known that I could not say no to him.

'You will do this for me?' he persisted.

All my future seemed to hang on that moment, and the dreadful part was that I knew it. There was the gurgle of the sterilizer, all the sounds of the home going on around us. I suppose that I wanted to see more of him, even then. I suppose that I loved him badly, a great deal more badly than I dared to admit even to myself.

You cannot stop that kind of love.

'I'll go with her,' I said, and I was keenly aware that my voice sounded unreal. I wondered if he noticed it, and only hoped that he didn't.

'Thank you, very much.'

I wondered if he knew how I was feeling, and what an effort it had been to accept, and then I told myself that he must not know, and whatever happened I must never let him guess about it. I had laid myself open to be very deeply hurt. I heard Sister on the stairs.

'Nurse,' she called.

That was the signal to return to duty.

Under a starched white apron no heart must be allowed to beat. There must be no sentiment, and there can be no time for love. Yet for all that, we nurses are women just as others, we feel as they do, we care as they do, and we suffer as they do.

Sister called me aside.

She said: 'It is your patient. She seems to be rather distressed; you see, I took her in a telegram and I think you ought to go in and see her.'

I went to Mrs. Harper at once. The room was a bower of flowers, all of them the more expensive kind; really, she must have had a host of generous friends. It was like entering some lovely springtime garden. She herself lay back among the pillows, and I was horrified to hear her sobbing. I went to her at once.

'You mustn't cry like that, you'll only hurt yourself,' I told her; 'there are the stitches to be remembered. Come now, Mrs. Harper, try to control yourself, you can't cry like that. What is the matter?'

But she went on.

After a frightful battle, I wheedled the trouble out of her, and it was of course all about Bill. I might have guessed that already! It seemed from what I could gather, but she was weeping so violently and making such a fuss that it was difficult to decipher what she said, that he had wired to her, and there was a very urgent message she must get back to him. And, whatever happens, Ray must never know.

'He just hates Bill,' she told me, 'he is the most unreasonable man; oh, he is cruel to me, so cruel.'

I didn't believe that, because cruelty was something outside Ray Harper's mentality. I had seen him when he had come to the home to carry out bad dressings, and had always been struck by his sympathy and tenderness and his care for his patient. A man who could behave like that, with such pity and kindness, was not the man who would be cruel to his wife.

I quite understood that he did not like the idea of Bill, whoever Bill might be, and yet I could not help remembering the perfect lilies which Ray had sent her and which she had thrust aside for Bill's basket of mimosa.

'Ray thinks that I have given Bill up,' she told me, and clung to me, 'he thinks the whole affair is over, and it will never be over. Never. Never. Never. Ray is so cold and reserved, and so desperately doctory, we ought never to have married.'

And only a few moments before I had looked into the eyes that were accused of being cold and reserved and had seen in them infinite care and compassion. They had held suffering too, and now I wondered if Flower was the person causing a great deal of that suffering. Then I pulled myself together, it doesn't do when a nurse starts wondering about her patient's private life. I was just the girl who was doing the nursing, and I told myself, pretty sharply, that I had better not forget it.

'I'll help you,' I promised, 'but you mustn't cry now. Just lie down and rest.'

It was imperative that she should not fling

herself about. The stitches were still in, and she might have done herself irreparable damage. It is a nurse's duty to help her patient to get well, and to soothe and comfort her if she becomes distressed. In hospital we are taught from the beginning that our first duty is always to the patient. Even if she is married to the man you love. Even if you are out of sympathy with her at heart. If necessary I would have to help Flower against Ray, and I knew it.

When I had got her calm again it was only to find that her temperature had gone up. Her pulse was erratic. I filled in the chart with some qualms because I was not too happy about her; I made my report to Sister.

'What has been happening?' asked Sister, and she read the report, and nibbled the end of the pencil, her brow knit, which meant that she was anxious, I knew.

'She received that telegram and it seemed to distress her very much.'

'Have you calmed her now?'

I nodded. I did not dare confess that the only way to calm her had been to consent to what she had wanted. The urgent message had got to be delivered personally, and she begged me to take a note round to a block of flats when I went off duty. I had not wanted to do it, at first I said flatly that I would do no such thing, but she had become so much more distressed and had been so hysterical, that in desperation I had agreed. I told her that George the porter would deliver it for her, but that did not satisfy her.

'Oh, you don't understand how important it is,' she kept crying, 'it must be you. You are the only one that I can trust.'

Eventually I promised.

She calmed down and said that she would try to sleep, and I went the round of the patients on that floor to relieve the other nurse. I had to get them ready for the night.

The girl next door was in a little cheap slip of a room and worried to death that she would not get well again in time to keep her job. I could not help thinking what a contrast she made to Flower Harper, with her masses of flowers and gifts, and this poor little soul who had absolutely nothing at all.

Further along the corridor was the young Padre with the broken leg. He had suffered a lot very bravely, and was so patient over it all that you felt proud to do any little thing you could for him.

I tidied him up, and just as I got out into the corridor again they were bringing a new patient up from the theatre. It was a girl, whimpering a little, with the first signs of returning consciousness; as she passed me by, Tenny beckoned to me as she walked at the head of the stretcher.

'Give me a hand at getting her into bed?' she said.

I ought to have been going off duty, but instead, I went into the room with Tenny. Screens surrounded the bed, and the lights were subdued. There was the smell of eau-de-Cologne, and by the side of the bed itself hyacinths, fat pink ones in a blue bowl.

'Her boy friend sent them along,' said Tenny, and she sniffed the air disapprovingly. 'Once I had a boy friend who sent me hyacinths. Heavens, how I hated them!'

'Hated them?' I said in surprise.

'Yes, *loathed* them. He was rather highbrow and was always quoting poetry about them.'

I nodded, I knew the verses that he had quoted, and gave them to her:

'If thou of fortune be bereft,
And of thy all but four pence left,
Buy bread with two, and with the dole
Buy hyacinths to ease thy soul.'

She crimsoned. 'Yes, that was it. Silly, I called it.'

And I had always thought it rather beautiful. But then, beauty strikes different ones of us in divers ways. It is something that cannot be analysed, something that cannot be actually placed.

From the bed there came a little cry, so that we both of us suddenly startled back to reality.

'Where am I? What's happened?'

It was I who turned to her. 'It is all over and you are safe back in bed again. Nothing to worry about. Lie quite still.'

Then I had to leave her. There was Flower Harper's note to be delivered. From the doorway I caught a last glimpse of her, banked up with pillows, and the scent of the eau-de-Cologne and the hyacinths mingling together. I knew she was going to be all right.

## CHAPTER TWO

# AT THE HOME

As I went down the stairs, I saw the night nurses coming on duty in a batch from below, fresh and white and light-hearted. Soon the bell would ring for our supper, and we would troop down like schoolchildren, and sit around the table headed by Miss Vaughan, who would enquire of each in turn as to what had happened.

'Well, and how's everybody?' asked Sister Bird, head night Sister, commonly known as Birdie.

'Grand.'

'And how's the new case on your floor, Nurse Day?'

'She's up from the theatre, just coming

round, and Tenny has got her in hand.'

'And your appendix?'

'Has a bit of a relapse and running a temperature, flew into a temper and did this for herself,' said I; 'but she is better now.'

'Doctor ordered a draught?'

I shook my head. 'He wants her to sleep naturally if she can; says if she is still restless at midnight she is to have a medinal.'

Birdie nodded as she jotted it all down in the case-book. 'These spoilt darlings,' said she; 'everybody gets whatever they want. You would think that it was almost worth while being ill, wouldn't you?'

'I'll take a last peep at her before I go off,' I said, and I slipped into her room. I knew that her husband would be in last thing to see how she was, and had had a horrid idea that I might run into him. Somehow I hated running into him. Yet I dare not avoid him. 'You promise me you'll try to sleep?' I asked her.

'Yes, Nurse, I will. Really I will,' but I did not like the look in her eyes.

'You will deliver that note?' she begged. I had already promised. I don't know if she thought that I was likely to go back on my word, or what it was, but I just nodded. I'd deliver it all right.

I went off duty.

What a relief it always is to feel that the day is over! Night nurses were rustling about in their quiet shoes, settling their patients off with hot drinks and fresh hot water-bottles. Nightcaps were going round, and in the hall a doctor was slipping into his coat and exchanging last remarks with the anæsthetist. There was the faint smell of the anæsthetic still hanging about him like an incense.

All the while during my supper I was regretting the fact that I had undertaken to deliver that letter for Mrs. Harper.

'You're very quiet, Nurse Day,' said Miss Vaughan from the head of the table.

There was never very much that she missed. She was one of those people who knew what you were feeling almost before you were aware of it yourself, which I suppose accounted for the fact that she had been such a marvellous nurse in her time.

I made the only excuse that I could think of. 'Oh, it has been rather a difficult day, and my head is aching a bit.'

It wasn't my head at all. The troublesome thing was that I knew quite well that I had had no right to undertake this commission for Flower Harper, but that I had been forced into a corner and had seen no other way of soothing her. He had said 'Take care of her; you will do this for me, won't you?' and he must have known that I would have done anything in the world for him.

Miss Vaughan said, 'I'm afraid that you have

got a rather difficult patient. Dr. Harper said that she wasn't easy when he rang up about her coming here, and I am proud that he should have chosen you. If your head aches, take a turn in the air after dinner. I know when I was nursing I always found that a little walk before going to bed made all the difference in the world.'

It really looked as though Fate were playing into my hand. I had been turning over in my own mind as to whether I could make an excuse to Mrs. Harper and explain that I hadn't delivered the note because I could not get out. Now Miss Vaughan was making the way clear for me. I glanced down the table. Twelve of us sitting there. Twelve white caps and tired faces above spruce white collars. Miss Vaughan, with her muslin cap and strings, presiding over the whole lot of us. All alike. All orderly. Sometimes being a nurse makes you want to be disorderly, and to stampede, or do something dreadful. It puts ideas into your mind.

Afterwards, when we had drunk our rather weak coffee, I went up to my room and put on my bonnet and cloak. It was all mad and ridiculous of me, but now I was determined to carry the thing through. I would deliver the letter, and, of course, nothing could happen to me, I told myself. I was just being silly! All the time I was conscious of a faint hammering inside my head. It really *was* aching now.

I went out into the street.

It was a lovely night. There was a moon and stars, and across the park there were the trees thickening already for buds. I don't know what there is about a starry night, but it has always made me feel dreadfully lonely, and that was how I felt now as I went across the square. It was the longing for somebody to share the evening with me; the longing for companionship. Daylight is never so intensely terribly lonely as is moonlight.

Dr. Harper would have gone upstairs to see his wife last thing. She was a lucky girl to have won a man like that, and she did not care for him in the way that I could have cared. I doubt if she had ever had it in her to love very deeply, because she was one of the new era of women, the kind that I have always found it rather hard to understand, who want all the gilding that life can offer, and none of the responsibilities. She was too erotic to stand everyday wear and tear. Marriage did not appeal to her, but love did, and that was why there was the affair with Bill which actually held her because it represented intrigue.

I found the block of flats easily enough. They were the expensive kind, and lots of the patients at the home had come to us from here. I know that the doctors sometimes said jokingly that the block was a little gold-mine to them.

I took the lift up.

'Captain Dawson?' I asked the lift-boy.

I thought that he looked at me rather doubtfully.

'Yes, miss,' he said, and then, as the lift was solemnly climbing up the shaft I caught him casting another curious look at me. It made me uneasy. I had never thought of there being something strange about this Bill who was such a friend of Flower Harper's.

He ushered me on to a small landing from which there were four flats branching off, and I rang the bell of the one that he indicated, which was marked with a small brass plate stating: *Captain Dawson.*

It seemed to be a long time before anyone came in reply, and eventually a man-servant answered, and seemed both sheepish and surprised to see me.

I gave him the note.

'I was to wait for an answer,' I said. It had been the answer which had worried my patient so much; she was crazy to get it, and all that I hoped was that it would be the answer she wanted when she did get it, or I would not be responsible for the consequences.

He surveyed it doubtfully and then admitted me inside the hall. I could see that he was suspicious and did not like having me inside the place at all.

'If you will wait there for a moment,' he said, and went off down a passage, leaving me standing where I was.

I don't think that I had ever been inside a bachelor's flat before. I sat down on a settle and stared about me. The place was done up in psuedo-Chinese style. It was mostly scarlet lacquer. There were dragons on the ceiling, and the cabinets had strange devices on them. In the tiny window there was a niche with an incense burner, from which there issued a dull smoke. The whole place seemed to be unreal and I was not impressed by it. But then that was hardly my affair, and anyway I had not liked my mission, and was possibly prepared to crab anything that I saw.

I sat down and started thinking about life in the home. Was I going on like this working for ever? A nurse's life is one of entire self-sacrifice; it means giving of herself, and in the end when she is too old for work, what happens to her? Walking between prim beds in hospital. Helping little new lives into the world, and old, tired lives out of it. I thought of the patients in the home, of the rooms that were like mirrors with eternal new reflections in them, new personalities passing through them. At one time an old lady, austere and dominating, who perhaps did not approve of flowers. Then a girl like Flower herself, spoilt and pampered, exquisite silk nighties, cobwebs of dressing-gowns, a long queue of adoring visitors. A man, too, who would perhaps not admit suffering and would be terribly brave. A child, frightened, yet sweet. All these passed through our rooms at the home, in a long string, and left impressions behind them.

That is the life of a nurse. Just a string of impressions, no more. And I wanted it to be more, I wanted the things that every girl hungers for, the love of a man to sustain you through life, a home, children of my own, something worth living for.

Suddenly the giver, whom I knew to be Bill, who had sent the golden basket of mimosa, appeared. He was tall and broad, in the gay twenties. His eyes were blue, with that cold, clear, steely blue which I always feel means cruelty. This may be a silly fancy of mine, but there is a hard blue like pebbles which seems to cut right through you. He was florid and fair. I suppose that most people looking at him would have said that he was a handsome man, but I am a nurse, and I read things into people's faces, things to which others may be blind.

I knew at once that he lived life hard. I thought that he drank too much—by that I don't mean that he was a drunkard, but that he was fond of good wine—and he was the kind of man who would have no idea of stinting himself. I disliked him intensely. I knew also by the way that he looked at me that he thought of me as a woman, never as a nurse, and that it was horrible.

He came forward.

'So you are Flower's nurse?' he said.

I tried to remain calm, but there was a feeling inside me that was anything but calm. I didn't like my errand, and I had no wish to be here at all. It was a place with an atmosphere; probably it was caused by the scarlet lacquer on the walls, and the queer smell of incense from the niche. Probably it was because I had a guilty feeling that neither Miss Vaughan nor Dr. Harper would have supported me in what I was doing.

'I am nursing Mrs. Harper,' I said, and I hoped very much that it sounded as cold as I meant it to sound.

'I see. When my man said that a nurse was here, I did not think for a moment that she would be so charming. Won't you come in and have a drink?'

'I don't drink.'

I felt irritated that he should look at me like that, in a way that made me feel cheap. And at the same moment I had a horrid idea that the very simplicity of my dress attracted him. He was used to women who dressed like Flower Harper, in cloth of gold, and lamé, in velvets and lovely shimmering satins. I had just my bonnet and cloak and the white apron over the mauve print frock under that cloak.

'I have been terribly inhospitable,' he said, 'very unkind. Won't you show me that you forgive me by accepting my hospitality now?'

I said that I was sorry and that I must get back. Could I have the note for which my patient was waiting, and I would return at once.

Then he looked at me and laughed.

He put out a hand and touched my cuff gently, and there was something about that touch which made me go a little cold. I do not mind what a man says to me—as a nurse I am used to plain facts—nor do I mind how he looks at me, but I have a fetish about being touched. I hate it. I kept telling myself that he was a bad lot, and that I had known it at once, perhaps from the very beginning, when Flower had talked about him. He had all the diabolical fascination of the bad man over the silly, erotic type of woman. But it was a fascination which was non-existent for me.

I brushed his hand aside and pulled myself up.

'Will you please give me the reply to the message?' I asked.

'Dear, dear. I'm sorry if I have offended you. Believe me, I did not intend that as anything but a compliment,' and he stood there, still looking at me.

I realized then that something would have to be done to end the interview.

'The note,' I repeated.

'Oh, yes, Mrs. Harper wants me to visit her at the home.

That made me start. I had never expected

this, because surely both of them must realize how dreadfully unfair such a visit would be to Ray Harper. He would be almost bound to hear of it, even if he did not come in and surprise them both. It was absurd to contemplate such a piece of folly. The doctor came in and out as he thought he would, sometimes quite early in the morning, sometimes quite late at night; it just depended when he was operating. He might so easily walk into the room and see them together, when he believed that Mrs. Harper had given Bill up. Surely no girl with a wonderful husband like Flower's could be long in love with anybody else, especially when the somebody else was like Bill.

'I think it would be very difficult for you if you tried to see Mrs. Harper in the home,' I said, and hoped he would take the hint.

'I see.'

'It would be most unwise,' I urged again, but he laughed at that.

'It might not be wise, but it would be very nice. I had thought myself that it would not be diplomatic, and I told her so. That was what she didn't like. But now, having met you, I have formed a different opinion of the home.'

Again there was that flicker in the blue eyes that were so hard, and the hand was stretched out involuntarily as though he would touch me again.

'Will you please give me the reply to that

message?' I asked him. 'Otherwise I shall have to go without it, and it will upset my patient very much. It is not good for her to be distressed while the stitches are still in.'

'You are very hard on a fellow.'

I fired up at that.

'I came here entirely against my own wishes, because Mrs. Harper had a crying attack, and she would have done herself serious harm. I promised the doctor that I would see after her, and coming to you personally was the only way to stop her.'

'Oh, yes, her husband. He is too strict with her. I don't wonder that she has crying attacks,' and he laughed. 'I suppose just because he is a doctor and has got some big reputation for himself as a surgeon, you think he is bound to be a hero? Nurses are like that.'

I wished he had not said it, because it was true. All of us at the home did think of him as being a hero. However, I wouldn't be drawn.

That was when he produced the letter. I suppose he saw that I did not intend waiting for it much longer.

'Thank you,' and I took it from him.

'Tell her that after I had written it I . . . I had reason to change my mind, and that I may be round to the home to see her. The day I intend calling I shall send her some white violets in the morning, then she will know. Letters are sometimes dangerous, aren't they?'

He twinkled. 'I dare say you have found that out already.'

White violets!

It sounded just like a schoolgirlish intrigue, and all the while she had a husband like Ray. I put the letter into my pocket, and drew my cloak closer about me. Bill was hateful. I was very glad to think that in a moment I could shut the door on him and go away, never to return to his flat. In future Flower Harper could manage her own affairs, and if she cried herself sick and made herself thoroughly ill over them, then that was her affair and not mine.

'That will be all, I suppose?' I said.

'You'll be seeing her to-night?'

'No, not to-night, her other nurse is with her now, and I do not go on duty again until seven-thirty in the morning.'

'So early?'

'So early,' I repeated.

He opened the door a little way, and as he did so took my hand in his and pressed it fast in his.

'Good-bye for a little while.'

I was so angry that I made no reply, but, feeling my face flush, I walked straight out and on to the small landing.

A man was standing outside the door of an adjacent flat, obviously waiting for an answer to his ring. I nearly collided with him as I marched out full of fury at the way I had been received.

'I beg your pardon,' I exclaimed as I saved

myself only in the nick of time.

The man turned. It was then that we recognized one another.

'*You?*' he demanded.

It was Ray Harper.

2

In that moment I saw through quite a lot of things, and realized that he must have been calling here to visit a patient, and that the door would open to admit him. I could not possibly give Flower away by explaining what I was doing here, and I saw him glance instinctively at the door which had closed behind me, and which had the brass plate with *Captain Dawson* on it.

He stared at me.

'Whatever are you doing here, Nurse?' he asked incredulously.

It happened to be one of those moments when I could say nothing at all. I tried to think of something, but thought would not clear itself, and words would not come. It seemed that the two of us stood staring at one another for ages, and I thought that it would never end. Then, when he spoke again, his voice was aloof, cold, and very distant.

'That is Captain Dawson's flat?'

I could not deny it, beside it would have been madness to lie with the name standing out there on the plate.

'Yes,' I said, and all the while there was the feeling inside me that I must think, I must find some excuse, only I just couldn't think.

'Did Flower send you to see him?' he asked quickly, and now his eyes were the eyes of the fighting man that I had seen above the white mask in the theatre of the home.

I prayed hard that the door might be opened before I had to answer that question, but of course it wasn't opened. He stood there staring at me, and I at him like a tongue-tied schoolgirl. What on earth could I do? I could not give my patient away, and I would not have hurt him for the world. I just did not answer.

'I see,' he said at last, and sighed, then he added, 'I asked you to do your best for her, and see after her for my sake, and now this happens.'

Still there was nothing that I could say; worse, there was nothing that I could think of to help us both.

Of course I had realized all along that he had known about Bill, and that he hated the man as I had done on sight. I wanted to be comforting. I wanted to help him and make him realize that I had not come here with the idea of cheating him, but of comforting Flower, and for all my good intentions there was nothing that I could say.

Then there came footsteps to the door of the flat where he was calling, and I heard somebody saying from within 'the doctor at last,' and, turning away, I actually ran down the stairs.

My face was stinging.

Naturally he thought that I had betrayed his confidence, he thought that I was acting as a go-between for Flower and her lover, and I had not been able to find my tongue, or to tell him the truth. What did I do next? What did I say next time I met him?

I wished I had never been called in to nurse her. If only I had had the courage to tell Miss Vaughan that I wouldn't, I should not have got myself caught up in this chain of circumstances.

Perhaps after this Dr. Harper might decide that I was not fit to be trusted with her, and would not go on persuading me to take her away. He might release me from my promise, and that would be a good thing.

All the way home I was seeing again the way that he had looked at me. It did not make me very happy. I was hearing the disappointment in his voice, and that hurt too.

I kept thinking what a mess you can make of life even with the best motives, and I was making a mess of it all right.

## 3

Next morning I saw the report book and learnt that Flower had had a bad night. She had taken her medinal at midnight and even then had had only a fitful sleep. The upset of the previous evening had retarded her convalescence quite a lot.

'She must not be disturbed by anything,' said Miss Vaughan, 'you must be prepared to pander to her on every score if you are to get her well.'

So that I could not tell her that I had had a horrible evening and had run into her husband outside the flat and that he suspected me. I could not tell her that nothing would make me act as a go-between any more, and she could send her own notes and take her own messages for all that I cared.

Instead I gave her Bill's message.

'He will send white violets the morning of the day that he is coming to see you,' I said primly, and thought what a silly message it was.

But it pleased her.

She smiled to herself as she lay among the pillows, and I suppose that the idea of white violets satisfied her sense of vanity.

'Dear Bill, he thinks of everything.'

I said nothing at all, because I did not want to get mixed up any further in this nasty business. She did not ask me questions, but let me get her ready for the day, watching me with far-away eyes. I think she was still a little dopey from the medinal, anyway she did not bother me with questions.

Tenny called me down the corridor to help her lift the operation patient who had come up last night. She was looking a great deal better this morning, and was lying there smiling at the bowl of hyacinths.

'I do hope that I wasn't a lot of trouble to you last night,' she said. 'I didn't quite know what I was doing and may have been crotchety.'

It is funny how some patients think such a lot for their nurses, while others never mind how much they worry you, believing that is what you are there for, and nothing else matters.

She was a plucky little kid, and had had a bad night too, but had stood up to the pain wonderfully.

'All grit and gold,' Birdie told Tenny when she came on duty.

We made her as comfy as we could, and she expressed the hope that the young man was coming along to see her; she was doing her best to perk up for him so that he shouldn't be worried about her.

'We are going to be married when I get well, Nurse,' she said. 'I only hope this illness doesn't make too big a hole in our expenses. We are thinking of every pound as one less table and chair,' and she laughed.

I rather wished that she was my patient, because she was such a dear little thing, the sort of little patient who makes nursing a pleasure.

Dr. Harper came to see his wife about eleven, in between two operations. I was putting her pillows straight and did not hear him come in until she spoke fretfully to him.

'You smell of anæsthetics, Ray, and make me feel quite ill.'

'Sorry, but I thought I had just time to run up and see how you were.' He stood there apologetically, and I was horribly aware that his eyes avoided mine. He was still angry with me about the previous night, still blaming me, I suppose.

I gathered up the flowers from her bedside table, and made them the excuse to leave her alone with him. Not once had he looked at me! I knew what he was feeling, but then I was feeling badly too, badly because it was such a dreadful misunderstanding, and I could not think what to say to put matters straight again.

When he came out of her room, I was in the nurses' sitting-room washing up some glasses. I could not believe it when I saw him peep round the corner of the door.

'She has rounded that corner well,' he said, 'and she seems a lot better this morning, though I shall be glad when those stitches are out. She tells me that her being like this is all thanks to you.'

I murmured something about having done nothing, and all the while I was sure that his eyes were trying to read what I was thinking.

He said, 'She is a queer little girl in lots of ways and she needs clever management. I can rely on you, can't I?'

'I will do my best, I promise you,' I said.

He still lingered and it occurred to me that he was waiting for an explanation of last night. Yet there was nothing that I could say. Apparently realizing that I was not going to speak, he turned on his heel. Downstairs the bell from the operating theatre burred. I saw a couple of nurses hurrying to the stairhead, and Sister coming in for the sterilized drum out of the sterilizer. The opportunity had passed and life had whirled us on again on its tide.

I ought to have told him the truth.

Or oughtn't I?

It is all very difficult to know, all very difficult to do. Opportunities do not come back to you in life. I know that. Yet perhaps it was all to the good that this had happened, because by going on with the affair, by nursing Mrs. Harper and by seeing him so often, I was only hurting myself badly, and getting nowhere. I was destined to go on with my nursing for ever, not to be somebody's beloved.

I decided then that I would tell him that I could not carry out my promise and go away for a holiday with his wife when she got better. He must forgive me but I just couldn't.

I went back to my floor just as the doors of the operating theatre shut to and the operation started below.

# 4

I was in charge of that floor for the entire afternoon.

I got my own tea in the sitting-room before taking down the patients', but even then you don't get much rest. I wanted to think, and to make some plans for my future, as to how I was going to break it to Dr. and Mrs. Harper that I couldn't go away with her, but all the time bells were ringing.

The little creature who had been operated on yesterday rang for me several times. She was thirsty, poor little soul. Then there was the man in number twenty-nine, who was worried about himself and needed soothing.

'Stay and talk to me, Nurse,' he implored, for his op. was in the morning and he was very agitated.

My own tea was cooling, but I could not be such a beast as to leave the poor fellow when he was so distressed.

Doctors were coming and going. The bell from the operating theatre went, and there was the sound of porters carrying stretchers up the stairs.

The life of a nursing home has to go on, whatever your own personal life may be, and eventually I went to bed tired out. All of me was absorbed in the home; it possessed me. Yet here, in my cubicle, I seemed to become an individual, somebody real and alive, and I wore a chiffon nightie, which he had bought and which Flower had given me.

As I tied the sash I thought how much I should have appreciated a husband who bought things like this for me. Flower did not care for him, but I knew that I could have loved him—if I dared. It was the eternal triangle.

I fell asleep and dreamed that he came to me and was sweet and tender, and that we were going to be married, and I woke to the sharp ringing of the nurse's bell, which meant hurried dressing and down to breakfast on the tick. You are allowed no licence, and the breakfast is a miserable affair, because nobody is anxious to start the day's work, and all the while you are aware that the night nurses are chafing to hurry you up and get you on duty, so that they may get a little relaxation after the long night.

Prayers too.

Prayers, and I did not *feel* like saying them. Somehow I felt that I had been wicked thinking about Ray Harper, when he was nothing to me and never could be. Probably he talked about me as 'that ham-faced nurse.' Doctors do, you know.

I went on duty with a heavy heart and did the round of my patients. It was when I had got the last one ready for the day that the porter brought up a little basket full of white violets for Mrs. Harper.

I went to the door and took it in.

'The messenger said that there wasn't a card,' he explained. 'He said that the lady would be sure to understand.'

Unfortunately I understood too.

White violets in a room already full of pink carnations and gold mimosa. A room which smelt of roses and lilies, and yet this fragrance borne by this little silver basket was ineffably lovely.

I showed them to her.

'They have come,' she said, and she dimpled. 'White violets. Oh, Nurse, that means that he will be here this afternoon.'

'I suppose so.'

But she did not notice me. She was wondering if the wave in her hair had kept sufficiently, and what she could put on her skin to make it look a little better. Then she became communicative and told me a little about her husband.

'Ray hates Bill,' she said, 'he simply can't stand him, and we have had some of the most dreadful quarrels about him already. If he comes here when Bill is with me, you will keep him outside, won't you?'

'I can't,' I said.

'Oh, but you can. You know you can.'

I stood at the end of her bed and tried to adopt a firm attitude with her. This wouldn't do. I was getting deeper and deeper into the mire, and I knew it. I explained, 'You are making it extremely difficult for me, Mrs. Harper, and I don't think you ought to ask me to do such things. A doctor has the right in this home to come in and see people. What could I tell him?'

She looked at me pitifully, and her lips began to droop. She was one of those people who cried very easily, and before I could say anything more the tears had begun. I knew it was dreadfully bad for her, yet the only way to comfort her was to tell her that I would do what she asked.

'You are so cruel to me,' she sobbed; 'you are one of those people who have never been in love yourself, and you don't know what it feels like.'

Never been in love myself! Don't know what it feels like! Hard words, with hard meanings, and quite wrong. But of course I could not tell her so.

'You will help me?' she whispered.

'I will always try to help you, but sometimes it isn't easy.'

'You could if you would. You could wait at the top of the stairs and catch Ray as he came up. He has got that patient in number fifty-one, you could make him go there first and then warn Bill about it.'

She had all the little mean intrigues at her finger-tips, had Flower. I might have guessed then that it wasn't the first time that she had stooped to this kind of thing, she was far too clever at it. I did not want to promise her anything. Doctors are not always too tractable, and I had seen a look in her husband's eyes that was very compelling.

I avoided it. 'I hate telling lies,' I told her. 'I hate cheating people, and I don't want to have anything to do with this. You don't seem to realize that I am in a bad position here. Supposing Miss Vaughan found out?'

'Oh, *that* old thing!' said Flower contemptuously.

'All the same she could dismiss me. And, if I start cheating the doctor, I deserve dismissal.'

Flower wept wretchedly. She sobbed, 'As if it would ever come to that! I never heard such nonsense. You might do it for my sake. I do think you might realize what I feel lying here, so miserable, and so alone.'

For her sake! And her husband had asked me to see after her for his sake. It was a very uncomfortable position for me, but I was determined that I would not promise to help her, however much she coaxed.

'I will do what I can, but I am promising nothing,' I said, and she had to be content with that.

It would not hurt Flower to find that she could not manage everybody who came into her life, and that she had not got the world at her feet as she thought. I contemplated teaching her a lesson.

# 5

We happened to have a bad morning that day.

They were operating as usual downstairs, and they were having a very difficult time with the patient. The operation went wrong. I heard that they were getting down extra help, and suddenly I was called off my floor and sent into the theatre.

To step into the theatre is like stepping into a world remote and distant from this. White figures, stertorous breathing, the tinkle of the anæsthetic and the heavy, sweet smell of it lying over everything. I have never got quite used to it, but still treat it with an awe and reverence of its own. In the theatre there is tension. Outwardly everything runs smoothly, there is never an order that is not carried out on the instant and exactly, there is never a fluster or a stir, but under it lies the strain, the agitated beating of hearts and the wonder at the miracle which gives life and hope and mends broken bodies and sends them back whole.

When I was ultimately returned upstairs it meant that I was behind with getting my lunch trays up, and I wanted to get my own patients settled for their nap before visiting hours started.

I got Flower Harper nestled down for a while, and then the porter came along with a card.

'A gentleman to see Mrs. Harper,' he said.

'These are not visiting hours. No one is supposed to come until three o'clock.'

Old George scratched his head thoughtfully. 'The gentlemen says that it is urgent. He said, "Get hold of her own particular nurse, she knows me and she will understand."'

I glanced down at the card and saw written on it: *Captain William Dawson*, which meant that I thoroughly understood. I was so angry with his impertinence that I determined to make him wait.

'Tell him that three o'clock is the visiting hour and that he must wait until the clock strikes,' I said. 'Show him into the waiting-room and he can wait there, or tell him to come back again, but she is asleep now and he cannot see her before the proper time.'

George went off, mumbling to himself. I don't think he relished giving the message.

I thought that there would probably be a quarrel about this when Flower got to know of it, but there was nothing of the sort. I went in just before three to tell her that he was waiting, and instantly she brightened up; I had to admit that she did look very lovely. She wanted to get herself tittivated for him. A filmy nightie, with an all lace top through which an exquisite pastel blue ribbon was threaded. Over it one of her pert little feather coats. There was no doubt about it, she was one of those lovely women who could wear lovely things with an air. She had her hair brushed until it shone like gold, and then insisted on rubbing it softly with a silk handkerchief. She smoothed a liquid powder over her cheeks while I held the mirror for her. A black pencil marked her eyebrows, and her mouth was warmed to vermilion by her lipstick.

'What about my cheeks, Nurse? Ought I to look pale but interesting? What ought I to do? I am wondering what will look best.'

And there were people on the same floor who were really ill! People who wanted so much to get better that they did not care how they looked. All this fuss for Bill. She would not have done it for her own husband.

Eventually she was settled and I was sent scuttling to the house 'phone to send down word that Captain Dawson was to come up.

I saw him arriving up in the lift and carrying a sheaf of flowers wrapped in tissue paper. I had to wait for him.

'This way!' I said curtly. I was very much on duty. I disapproved of his visit, seeing all that he meant to her, and how much he would have hurt Dr. Harper, and I did not care if he realized how I felt.

'I say,' he said, 'you have forgiven me for the other night, haven't you?'

'We won't discuss it,' I told him.

'One minute before I go in. I know that you have been awfully good to Flower; she is full of all that you have done for her, and it was nice of you bringing me that message. As I came down Bond Street I saw this little trinket, and wondered if you would like it. My arms are awfully full with these flowers, so do relieve me of it?'

He held out a small jeweller's box, and on the lid there was inscribed a magic name, the sort of name that girls dream about and too seldom find on their own belongings. I knew that inside there was some fascinating gift, something that, if once I saw it, I should want to keep desperately for my own.

The whole of my life I have never had pretty things. I have been extremely hard up. My people were hard up before me, and all my youth had to a large extent to be shorn of its trimmings. I am not the type to whom people give pretty gifts. My patients nearly always send me a serviceable handbag, neat hem-stitched hankies, something which, as they (to me, rather tragically) put it, 'looks like you.'

I handed the box back.

'I am afraid that it is against our rules for a nurse to accept presents in this way,' I said, and so that there should be no more ado, I brushed past him and on into Flower's room.

'Here is someone to see you,' I said.

Then I left them alone.

# 6

I brought the flowers out with me to arrange them into vases for her. They were perfect. Here were white lilac and Spanish irises mingling together with the snow of whiteness and the spires of soft blue and mauve.

'She is a lucky girl,' said Tenny, passing me on the way to one of her patients, 'she doesn't know when she is well off.'

'She seems to have got most of the things that she wants.'

'Most of them? I should think that she has! Married to that marvellous man for one thing! and then to have boy friends as well.'

'You have boy friends,' I reminded her, for Tenny was pretty as a picture.

Instantly her face clouded.

'There was one, and it seems to me that he was her sort too, the sort that never means anything by it. He was gay, just like that. He used to bring me flowers and then one day he deserted me when I was in the most dreadful trouble. Never again, thank you. No more boys for me,' and she went on her way.

Somehow I felt that I had pried in upon some intimate part of poor Tenny's life, something that still hurt her, and I niched in my mind the reminder that I must not talk about boy friends again. Tenny had once had a bad let-down.

I arranged the flowers, taking as long as I could, and then I went back with them to

Flower's room. Captain Dawson was sitting beside the bed holding her hand, and I knew by his face that he had been making love to her. She looked enchanted as she lay there. Silly little Flower! Stupid little Flower—and with Ray for a husband, too!

When I went back to my post on the landing my heart was heavy, and I knew that I should not be happy until the Captain had gone again. I heard the bell go; they rang it three times on our landing to tell us that a doctor was on his way up. Somehow I guessed who it was, and I thought, 'This is sheer bad luck again. He will think that I am trying to cheat him and yet what can I do about it?'

I wasn't going to risk anything else, and I whisked into Flower's room.

I burst in upon them both so quickly, that I found Bill with his head on her pillow, and his hand holdings hers fast.

'Quickly,' I said, 'a doctor is coming up the stairs, and it may be Dr. Harper. Captain Dawson had better slip into the nurses' sitting-room and wait there for a few minutes.'

It was the only thing that I could think of, and you may be sure it was not because I had any sentimental feelings for him. They had been going to argue, but I would have none of it, and I bustled him out pretty fast. It was only just in time, too! I got him pushed into our sitting-room, and shut the door, turning to meet Ray Harper coming up the last flight.

'These stairs!' said he and he laughed, 'I must be getting an old man, for they knock all the stuffing out of me.'

'Everybody gets puffed on them,' said I.

My own heart was hammering so hard that I was afraid that he would hear it, though outwardly I suppose I looked calm enough. A nurse's uniform helps in that. Prim. Starched. Aloof. Anyway he did not seem to notice anything amiss. We stood there in the alcove which is at the stair head, with the tea-trays laid on the side table, and the drip of a tap from the distance.

'How is she to-day?'

'She is much better. Her temperature is keeping down beautifully.'

'We don't want any more relapses. She is highly strung and emotional, you know, and takes things to heart. She lives on her nervous energy. She gives way easily and then flops. You will take care of her, won't you?' he added.

'I am doing all I can.'

A look passed across his eyes, as though he felt that I was offended, then suddenly he put out a hand, a hand slender like a woman's with finely pencilled fingers, the hand of a wonderful surgeon.

'You know I don't mean it that way. You know that I have infinite faith in you. I knew the first time that I ever saw you that you were a great woman.'

A great woman!

I wondered for a moment if he were laughing at me, and then I dismissed the idea and choked down the longing to cry, the keen desire to hide my face in my two hands in case my eyes should admit the truth.

I was taking care of her for him. But it was costing me far more than I liked to admit. I wanted to say then and there, 'There is a man hidden in the nurses' sitting-room, and it is the man you hate and have forbidden her to see again. Can't you do *anything* about it?' But I could not.

Making mischief would not help any of us very much, and I knew that. He stood there staring at me, as though he had forgotten time, and was thinking something which I could not fathom. I think I knew then, perhaps for the first time, that he had thought of me a little when he had been away from me. I think I was frightened, afraid lest this should go further, it was something that was too big for me, and which, once it escaped me, might hurt more than I liked to think.

He turned and went to her room.

'What lovely white violets! Where did you get them?' was the very first thing that he asked.

I closed the door on him discreetly. After all, it was only fair, even if she were ill, that she should get herself out of her own scrapes. I hated seeing him so cheated, so blind to her shallowness because he himself was so much in love. When you care for anybody it complicates life enormously, and it is almost worse for a nurse, who should behave like a machine, her stiff starched uniform, and her face trained so that never a flicker passes across it.

Very often she has to inflict pain that actually hurts herself too, but the patients only think that she is hard-hearted and cruel; they do not seem to realize that under it all she is also a woman and may suffer herself.

I thought as I closed the door upon the two of them that I could not bear this much longer. I'd do something desperate. I'd resign my post and go away, right away into the blue. Then I told myself not to be such a little fool; posts like the one at Miss Vaughan's are not to be picked up on blackberry bushes, and I had done awfully well to get into the home at all. To throw it aside because I happened to have felt foolishly about Ray was an incredible piece of folly which I should regret all my life.

I thought of Ray in his white coat and mask working against time in the theatre, a man with a set face and with his eyes showing his determination. I thought of him as he had been just a few minutes previously, standing in the niche and touching my sleeve. Surely he would not have done that if he had not thought about me?

Ray, the first time that we had met, doing that intricate operation, fighting for his patient's life. Ray, with only his eyes showing, yet those eyes telling so much. Yet here he was now deluded and tricked by his own wife, and I hated it.

I went back to the nurses' sitting-room, very small and snug, and I saw Captain Dawson sitting in the one easy chair.

He got up as I came in.

'Is the old man likely to be long?' he asked.

I resented his speaking of the doctor like that, and I dare say I showed it.

'You mean Dr. Harper?'

'You're very professional, aren't you?'

I disregarded his flippancy and the way that he looked at me with amusement, because everything that he did made me childishly angry. He was flauntingly impertinent, although he never said anything that was actually impertinent; it was more the manner in which he said it.

'The doctor usually stays about half an hour.'

'Oh, Lord!' Down he sat again.

I tried to forget he was there and went about the little sitting-room putting on the kettle for tea, yet horribly aware that he was eyeing me.

At last he spoke.

'I say, I do wish you would relieve me of this beastly little box.'

I did not attempt to parry it, but told him

quite plainly that we were not allowed to receive gifts like that.

'No, but rules are only made to be broken. You could waive the point, and you know that. Won't you do it for me?'

'Certainly not.'

He gave a sigh and put the box back into his pocket again; it seems absurd to admit it, but I was aching to know what he had got inside it, only I realized that it would have been fatal to look closer.

He started in a new vein.

'Flower looks fine. It is all your nursing, so she says. It was your nursing that brought me along to-day. You know, I had made up my mind to break off the affair and never to see her again.'

I did not want to go into these very private details of their personal affairs, and I said so.

'I wish you wouldn't tell me these things.'

I believe he had tried to lead me into saying that, for now he ignored it.

'When you came with that message I felt differently. You know, Nurse, if I had not given you that letter myself I should never have come round here to-day. Not on your life. It was just that I was itching to see you again.'

'I'm sorry you troubled yourself to come.'

He was the type of man who flirts with anything in a skirt. The sort of man who simply has to make love or he isn't satisfied.

'You're being very cold to me.'

'Well, what else do you expect?'

'You must be interested in me, or you would not take the trouble to hide me here so that the irate husband does not catch me. You help Flower . . .'

I rounded on him then.

'A nurse's duty is to her patient. She is in that state now when it would be quite wrong to allow her to cry or to upset herself in any way. She tried to have a relapse the other night, and I have a certain duty to perform, which I am performing, but only to the limit of that duty.'

'By George!' said he, and then, 'What a little spitfire it is!'

You could not do anything with him.

I went on with the trays, and all the time I tried to pretend that he was not here at all, and to keep my ear on sounds from Flower's room. Would Ray never go? And, what was worse, I was now worried to death that he would come down the landing to have a word with me before he finally left. If so, he would be sure to see Captain Dawson sitting here, and would think that maybe he had come to see me.

Then I heard Tenny coming along.

'Tea for the troubadour,' she called gaily from outside. 'Tea for the hungry! Open the door for me, Dallas; I've got my hands full.'

As I opened the door I caught sight of Captain Dawson's face. It had gone sheet-white.

I thought that the man must be going to faint, but I had no time to do anything about it.

The door swung open, and there was Tenny, with her little white cap perched on her hair, and her merry eyes laughing above the great tea-tray that she held. She took one look into the room, and then, seeing me, she dropped the complete tray in a heap. It made a sound like one of the big guns.

Then she turned on me.

'How did Bill get here?' she demanded.

Two of us standing there in the doorway, two of us, not knowing what had happened, and between us the fragments on the floor, the broken china, and the tea seeping away on to the linoleum. I had no idea what it was all about.

## 7

I think that my memory of what happened next is all very confused. I know that I heard a murmur from behind me, and realized that Captain Dawson was making some excuse as he got up and went out. He stepped across the débris on the floor, and we were both of us too disturbed to stop him.

I was listening to hear if Sister had heard the crash; it would, of course, be that dreadfully starchy Sister Johnson on duty, one of those women who can never forgive anything, and we should never hear the end of this if she came up.

Apparently she had not heard it.

Captain Dawson went across the landing and down the stairs. I think that I had been too horrified by the smash to worry whether he would run into Ray Harper. I think I had forgotten everything save that almost all of a tea-service had gone, and that Tenny was standing against the door, not making any attempt to cover her tracks, but staring helplessly into space.

There must have been something between these two, something that I did not know about; something hidden away in that part of Tenny's life at which she had hinted vaguely from time to time. It was a shadowy part. Though she was such a bright little person and so gay, I had always known that she had had suffering and difficulty and that there had been something which she kept from everybody.

Well, Captain Dawson had gone down the stairs before you could say Jack Robinson, and there were Tenny and I with the cups smashed to bits on the floor between us. At any moment Sister might come up the stairs and catch us. And Tenny was doing nothing about it. I dropped to my knees and began picking up pieces.

'That man,' said Tenny, and she began to cry half hysterically.

She went forward into the sitting-room and

sat down at the little table there, with her head flopped forward into her hands. I had never seen her in such a state of collapse before.

'That awful man! And I thought that the whole thing was dead and done with. I thought it was all over for ever, and it isn't. I don't believe that anything is dead and done with.'

She went on sobbing.

I was still on the floor trying to shovel the bits out of sight in case Sister suddenly appeared from nowhere, for she was one of those women. I bundled them back on to the tray and rang down for the food lift to send up another tea. It was not till then, when I had more or less covered all tracks of the accident, that I could go across to Tenny and take her hand.

'Tenny, my dear, what has happened? What was it? Tell me all about it?'

She turned on me instantly and challenged me quite sharply.

'You brought him here?'

'I brought him into this room, yes, but he isn't a friend of mine; he is a friend of Mrs. Harper's.'

'*Her* friend?' Tenny was twisting a wet little wisp of a hankie round her fingers. 'But he couldn't be anybody's friend. Listen to me, Dallas. He was the man I knew before. He came to visit somebody in the hospital where I was working, and we fell for one another. Oh, I dare say it sounds ridiculous to you, but he is the kind who sweeps you off your feet. I used to go out and see him; he was terribly nice to me and took me out on my days off. He gave me chocolates, great big boxes of them, and flowers, always the most expensive kind. I remembered him for ever by the white violets that he used to send me. No other man in the world would ever think of sending a girl white violets.'

I thought of this morning and the little silver basket full of them which he had sent to Flower, and the silly sentimental message that they carried her, saying that he was coming to see her. So he had played with poor little Tenny the same way, too!

I said, 'But that is all forgotten now, Tenny dear?'

She shook her head.

'No, there are some things that you can't forget. We got engaged; it was to be a secret and nobody would know about it ever. Then one night we went for a motor ride. We went down to Hindhead—such a lovely starry night, it was. He was wonderful and so kind to me. He said all the adorable things that girls ache to hear a man say. He had a way of kissing you—oh, it sounds silly enough now, but it was something that you could not resist. It was something that made you forget that there had ever been a time before or that there was ever going to be a time after.'

The fresh tea came up, carried by George the porter.

'Been a h'accident?' he asked, and when I nodded, 'My, there'll be a rumpus when that Sister knows!'

I said, 'She isn't going to know if I can help it,' and George, who is an awfully good sort, took the bits down in his food lift so that I breathed freely for the first time and hoped that was another hurdle safely crossed.

Tenny went on: 'We stayed there late and the car broke down. Now it seems to be such a silly stereotyped old story, but it did not seem to be silly at the time. I don't suppose such things do. We stayed the night at a hotel he knew of, and oh, Dallas, you mustn't think too badly of me. I don't know how it happened, but it just did. You see, we were going to be married soon, he said, and nobody would ever know. I dare say I behaved badly, but I defy any girl to have been alone in the country with the man of her choice on a night like that and not to be carried away. I could not regret it in the morning either. I dare say you think me wicked, but this was something from which you cannot escape.'

I thought of Dr. Harper; I know I had no right to do so, but I did. I knew what it would have been like if such a thing had been possible . . . of course, it wasn't, and never would be . . . but that was how I pictured it. I nodded.

She went on brokenly:

'Afterwards he started cooling off. The white violets did not come any more. Once he had told me that if ever he fell out of love he would never have the heart to tell me bang out, but would do it by sending me hyacinths. Don't you remember the other day when I said I hated hyacinths? It was because of Bill. He is a man with the most queer whims and fancies, and he has the most queer ways with flowers. He said if ever you receive white hyacinths from me, you'll know that it is the end.'

'And he sent them?'

'Yes, he sent them all right! It was just at a time when I felt queer and awful. I felt that I could not drag myself about because I was so worried. I felt terrible. I was frightened to go to a doctor in case it was the worst—frightened of the consequence of my own folly, and yet I couldn't do anything about it. I went on trying to blind myself to it, and it was awful, Dallas, just frightful.'

'But why didn't you tell Bill?'

'I did. I wrote to him and begged him to come to see me, only he had gone for a holiday. I got funky and dared not write the words that worried me. I wanted to creep into his arms and tell him and hear him put everything right. I tried to convey all my anxiety between the lines, but I don't suppose that it made much difference. I seemed to go on changing. I was fighting against that change all the time, but somehow it didn't work. Then I knew that I was going to have a baby.'

'Oh, Tenny, how awful!'

She stared at me hopelessly. 'It was worse than awful. I have often thought how dreadful it must be to be condemned to death and to wait in your cell for that last journey out into the light. Well, I felt that way. I knew that I was in a blind alley and that there wasn't any other way out. Like a rat in a trap. People who have not been in that position don't understand how horrible it is. I kept telling myself that the moment Bill got back he would put everything straight and marry me right away.'

I poured out the tea and handed her a cup. She took it automatically; I don't think she even realized what it was, she was so worked up.

'Then I got that horrid sick feeling with wondering supposing that he didn't come and see me, and insist on marriage. I expect in my heart all along I had known that he was a rotter, I had never deceived my real self, and now I was terrified. I heard suddenly that he had been back for over a week and had never sent me a word. That hurt. One of the other nurses had seen him and she told me about it.'

She sat there very still for a moment, and I persuaded her to have some tea. All the time I was wondering what was going on in Flower's room. Surely Dr. Harper would have gone by now? I hoped they were not arguing, or that he had not suspected Bill Dawson being there. Then my mind came back to Tenny.

'I had implored him to come to me the moment that he got home, or if this were impossible to let me go to him. So when I knew he was back I went round to his flat. There was some other girl there; I knew that the moment the man-servant opened the door to me, because I could see her bag and gloves in the hall, and I thought then that I should have gone mad about it. I couldn't get inside. He wrote to me at once, a very stiff and formal letter, saying that I had put him in a most embarrassing position by going round like that, and I mustn't do it again, whatever happened. I suppose I lost my head; it isn't easy to keep it when you are going to have a baby, and I was quite frantic by this time. I wrote and told him the truth, and said that he must do something to help me. He must arrange our marriage before anybody else knew. There was Matron, who had the eye of a hawk, and all those sisters watching me all the time. Oh, Dallas, I was so frightened! He wrote back and said that he did not know what on earth I meant, and, anyway, he could not be responsible.'

She began to cry again rather desperately. I felt as though she was ripping open a scar, something that hurt most terribly.

'What did you do?' I asked.

There was not much that she could have

done, poor child, so hideously alone.

'I wrote again, and begged him to help me, hating myself and hating him too. I don't quite know what I said because I was so utterly distracted. What do wretched girls do when this sort of thing happens to them? You can't have any idea how horrified I was, what a nightmare it seemed to be, and then in the middle of it all he sent me a bunch of white hyacinths.'

I think that I personally have always loved white hyacinths, but I knew then that they had suddenly lost their sweetness for me for ever. I would never see them again but what I should think of the agony that poor little Tenny must have suffered at that particular moment when she opened the box and saw the flowers lying there.

'And then?' I asked.

There was no sound of Sister's starched dress on the stair. There was only the light buzz of conversation in the rooms where patients had visitors. Only the high essence of flowers blown across the landing, and with it the faint smell of disinfectants which hung about the theatre below.

'And then?' I repeated.

She mopped her eyes. 'I'm a beast to worry you with this story. It is all over and done with now. It doesn't matter any more, it doesn't hurt any more, which is one thing. When I saw those white hyacinths I knew that he had never meant to marry me, and having got all that he wanted, was going to quit. The car had never broken down at Hindhead; it is just that one is so blind when one falls in love. The whole thing had been prearranged. I fainted then, and when I came round I was really ill. Mercifully the whole thing put an end to what I had feared, but I had learnt a dreadful lesson, much worse than anything I could ever have imagined. After that I gave up all my old friends, went away and started again, forgetting the old associations. I'm gay now, and I enjoy my fun, but I'm careful and I'd never trust any man in the world. Although I laugh about it, I wouldn't even trust anyone like Dr. Harper.'

'Dr. Harper?' I repeated, dismayed that she should have followed my own thoughts so closely.

'No, I wouldn't! I wouldn't trust any man. I know what they are. I thought that I would never see Bill again and that he had gone out of my life for ever, but he hasn't. He wasn't here talking to you, Dallas? You were not believing his stories?'

'I told you no. He came to see Mrs. Harper, and when the doctor came I popped him in here because there was nowhere else to put him. I don't like him.'

She shook her head a trifle wearily, as though she grasped something which I had not yet understood.

'It is because you do not know how fascinating he can be. That is all,' she said.

## 8

A bell rang.

'Goodness, I can't answer it like this,' gasped Tenny, and she tried to repair some of the ravages the tears had made on her face.

'I'll go.'

It was the latest operation case asking for a drink, a poor little bit of a body sunk in between hills of pillows, a forlorn little soul, and you could not help but feel sorry for her. Yet when I gave her the glass of water she made a little face, because it tasted horrible, as I had guessed it might. I shook up the pillows and tried to put her a little more comfy; all the while her eyes watched me.

'You nurses are rather like angels, aren't you? The way you watch over folks, and do things for them,' and she tried to smile.

'I'm not much of an angel.'

'You looked awfully like one to me when you gave me that drink,' she said.

'You'll be better to-morrow,' I promised her, and left her hoping that she would doze. You can't help feeling sorry for people coming round from an op. The minutes seem an eternity, and to-morrow so far away.

As I came out of her room, closing the door softly behind me, I found Dr. Harper on the landing. He turned to me at once, and I knew by his manner that something was amiss. I wanted to get back to Tenny, and was hoping and praying Sister would not come popping up and catch her with those red swollen eyes of hers.

'I wanted a word with you, Nurse. My wife's better, you've done a lot for her, you know.'

'Not very much.'

'She isn't easy to deal with, and everything has depended largely on her nurse understanding her. Now she is making excellent progress and she ought to be fit to leave the home and go away for her change soon.' He paused, and then he looked directly at me. 'It has made me tremendously happy to know that you are going to be with her.'

Up till this moment I had been making up my mind that I would break it to them both that I could not go away with her. I wanted badly to get out of it, but when he stood there looking directly at me, and saying it in that humbly grateful voice of his, I couldn't do anything about it. He smiled at me, and then he went on. I might have known that he hadn't finished yet.

'Look here, I've got to ask a favour of you. If anything should go wrong whilst you two are away, I want you to promise to send for me immediately, whatever Flower says to the contrary. Although I shall be down to see her in the week-ends, Monday till Friday is rather a long time stretching in between, and I want to be quite certain that you will see after her for me.'

'But she will be quite all right,' I promised him. It is so queer how doctors always think that their own are going to get some rare relapse. Mrs. Harper had had quite an ordinary appendix, and had been on the table a record short time; it was extremely unlikely now that she would have anything go wrong. To-morrow her stitches would be out, after that it was all plain sailing and there was nothing to worry about.

He said: 'I don't mean that. It isn't her health that is worrying me. It is . . .' For a moment he seemed undecided as to whether not to tell me something which went against the grain to repeat or whether to let me wholly into his confidence. Then he broke down that last boundary of reserve. 'I can trust you, Dallas?'—that was when I knew that I had ceased to be 'Nurse' to him for ever.

'Of course.'

'It is no good glossing over the fact that Flower and I have not made too big a success of our marriage, though Heaven knows I have wanted to keep that dark. She has different standards, it isn't her fault, but I am a sombre old stick and she is rather the gay butterfly type. It is probably all my fault and I accept and bear the blame, but I am so hoping that now perhaps things are going to be different. I once hoped that we should have children, and that they would make things better, but Flower hates babies. Perhaps it is just as well, because most people suffer a lot in this world, you and I in our calling ought to know that, and it seems almost cruel to bring others to it to go on suffering, doesn't it?'

I did not know what made him talk this way and was shocked at the sudden picture I got of him, the man as he really was, full of pain. I couldn't go on pretending about it when he looked like that, and I knew that I was caring more for him every day. It wasn't any use fighting against an emotion like that because it swept me along willy-nilly, and I was powerless to fight against it. It seemed to be all wrong, for only the other side of the door he had closed behind him lay his wife, and she did not care for him at all.

Hadn't she told me as much? I was torn two ways and I knew then that the way of the man whom I cared for must be the one I trod in the end. I think we both realized that in the one moment we had passed a milestone in our lives, because he put out a hand and laid it on mine with a little gesture of confidence. The feeling of that hand made me want to break down, to run away, to escape for ever, and all the while I stood firm, and tried to pretend to myself that I was a fool and dreaming all this; it was something that wasn't true, that wasn't real.

He went on quickly. 'I've got to take you into my confidence. God knows that this looks like giving my wife away, and that is the last thing that I ever want to do, but I don't want her to see any more of that Captain Dawson. You may think me a prude, but I was frankly horrified to see you at his flat last night. I don't want that to happen again, because whatever you may say I have a very shrewd idea of how you got there.'

I was horribly embarrassed.

I felt myself swaying between two courses, and then I remembered dear old Matron at the hospital where I had trained. Matron coming between the prim rows of beds, and in those beds patients in little red flannel jackets, and with white peaky faces. Matron, a grand old lady, even if she was a bit of a Tartar, and Heaven knows that she was all that, standing by my side and talking to me about the profession into which I had just recently been admitted. 'A nurse's first duty is to her patient; never forget that, Nurse. Your patient must always be your first consideration. Nobody else matters.'

So I said nothing.

He went on: 'She mustn't see any more of that man, he turns her head and he isn't a decent fellow, she will only be hurt by such a friendship in the end. Do you understand that?'

I said, 'Very good,' but I knew that my voice

was husky.

All the while, almost as though he had forgotten it, his hand rested on mine, and I could feel those tremendously strong fingers which had so often, as though by a sheer miracle, done such marvellous work in the theatre.

'You'll take good care of her, won't you?' and then, 'I know that you are keeping something back from me and I do so wish you would drop this veneer and open your heart to me. I wish you'd tell me the truth. I tell you the truth, you know.'

I knew that.

He stood waiting there, as though almost expecting me to say something more, and then, last of all, in a voice which had dropped a tone, 'The first time I saw you I felt that you were my friend. Why don't you behave as my friend, Dallas?'

Then he turned and left me.

I stood there staring after him. So he had thought about me, so he had looked upon me as being a friend, and he thought that I was not behaving squarely by him. As though I did not want to open my heart to him and tell him everything, yet how could I? The other side of the door was a great bowl of white violets with the idiotic message that had been sent to her by them, and which nobody else understood. Only a few minutes ago Captain Dawson himself had bolted down the staircase to avoid Tenny, to whom he had sent that cruel bunch of white hyacinths.

A nurse's first duty! . . .

The words spun round in my head and I wanted to admit the truth, but I dare not. My hand still burnt with the feeling of his upon it. I was love-sick as any silly schoolgirl, and I in my position as a nurse who had got past the stupid stage when they believe that every doctor is in love with them.

I gave myself a shake.

The operating theatre bell jarring through the floor brought me back to life with a start, and I bumped down to earth. The theatre Sister had come to the head of the stairs, looking washed-out and tired. Her cap was awry and, seeing me, she sank down exhausted into the one chair.

'Oh, we've had such an awful time,' she said, 'the poor chap collapsed on the table, literally stopped breathing. I wish Dr. Harper had been doing the op. You feel so safe with him; it was Treeves Spencer, you know, and he always gets so flustered and is so rude to the nurses. Oh, we have all been capering round on thorns.'

'Come and have a cup of tea in the nurses' room?' I suggested.

From up the stairs there came the smell of disinfectants and the heavy sweet essence of anæsthetic. It clung to her clothes, as she followed me into our sitting-room and slumped down heavily into a chair.

'I don't suppose he'll last out the night, but anyway that has finished my duty for the day. I'll never get used to that happening! I'll never become accustomed to it, and with Treeves Spencer too, what a frightful man he is!'

Tenny had recovered. Looking at her now, you would never have guessed that she had broken down so badly earlier in the day. She was her old brisk self.

'Oh, he'll be all right,' she said, 'he'll keep his nurses going all night, and probably demand fried eggs and bacon for breakfast in the morning. I know his sort!'

I left them there comparing notes. After all I had been away from Flower for a long time and I owed her some of my minutes. The moment I popped my head round the door, she turned and smiled.

'Is Bill still here?'

Her first thoughts were for him.

'He has gone, he stayed in the nurses' little room for a bit and then he ran off.'

I wished that I dared tell her the truth, but I dared not. For one thing I don't suppose that she would have believed me; women in love never believe anything against the beloved; and for another it would only have made her hate me. It was no consolation to know that if Flower bored Bill he would have no compunction in sending her white hyacinths as the gentle hint that he was through with her. He was that sort of man, but her silly eyes were blinded to it.

She held out a little dressing-jacket that lay on the bed, a soft fluffy affair, lined with silk.

'Poor Ray, he tries so hard, but he just has no ideas.'

'I think you are very unkind about him.'

She dropped the dressing-jacket and her mouth slowly opened.

'You think that? Why, though they say that he has never had a nurse nurse for him who didn't fall in love with him, I never thought that of you. Are you in love with him? How very odd! How very queer! You of all people!'

'Don't be silly,' I snapped, and it was idiotic of me because turning snappy did not help me, and only made her surer that she had smelt the truth out.

She said: 'I can assure you that Ray is definitely cold where women are concerned. He has had too many after him, he has been spoilt. He is the coldest fish in this world; I'm his wife and ought to know.'

'Please don't let's discuss him.'

'Oh, very well, as you will,' and she laughed again to herself. 'Now Bill has ideas! Ray would send me lilies, a flower you can buy at any shop, but it would be Bill who would get me white violets and send them. He is the only man in the world who would think of white violets.'

Just what Tenny had said! And Bill would also think of white hyacinths. I wanted to give her a good talking-to, but of course she had still got those stitches in and it wouldn't have been very fair of me. Somehow I felt my patience with her ebbing. She wasn't right about her husband, she wasn't truthful. To-night just outside her door I had felt his hand possessively on my own and had seen his eyes. He wasn't cold. He wasn't the type she described. He really had deep feelings, and she had just bruised those feelings to the extent that he had to admit that their love was a failure.

It was a dreadful mix-up.

'We are going to the sea almost at once,' she said, 'to Ventnor. It will be warm sunshine and flowers there and a Riviera-like atmosphere, so Ray says, and he can get down for the week-ends.'

'I hope Captain Dawson won't be there for the weeks,' I reminded her. It was mean of me, but I could not resist letting fly that barb. She deserved it anyway.

She raised those thinly plucked eyebrows of hers.

'Of course not. And anyway, even if he did why shouldn't he stay where he likes? It's a free country and hotels are public, anybody can stay in them.'

I knew that she was irritated, and only hoped

that I had not hit the nail on the head, though I might have guessed that I had done.

It wasn't a particularly happy thought.

She did not say any more, though I knew that she was bottling it all up, because she watched me all the time. I was taking the flowers out for the night. Tall crystal vases of roses, the long-stemmed variety. Lilies with their heavy scent, carnations in sheaves. I have never known any girl to have so many flowers when she was ill.

Last of all she had to say something.

'I only hope you aren't going to start butting in on my life, Nurse,' she said a little peevishly. 'Bill can come down to Ventnor if he wants to. Ray would not want me to be miserable there. It is most important that I should be happy.'

I said nothing.

I might have guessed that this was what she was warming up for. I might have known what the trouble was all about. He and she had arranged it all very neatly, and now they wanted me to be their ally.

I went on carrying out the flowers, and all the time she was watching me furtively from under her brows. I knew that she was thinking all sorts of things about me, whether I was to be got round, or whether I was going to be obstinate about this. I gave her no indication of my inward feelings at all. Why should I? I felt thoroughly angry with her. I was intensely angry that she could behave in this way when she was married to a man like her husband. Ray was forbearing and patient. It does seem hard in this world that the good husbands seem always to get the bad wives. You see a lot of it in hospitals and homes, for there you come into contact with the more intimate side of people's lives, and know them themselves really better.

She went on watching, and last thing of all when I was just going off duty she called me back, and clung to my wrist and became quite hysterical.

'You aren't angry with me?' she begged. 'Please, please don't be angry with me.'

And of course I had to make it up with her, and pretend that I agreed with all she said just to soothe her down.

This can't go on, I told myself, it isn't good enough. I must do something to stop it.

## CHAPTER THREE

# LIFE BECOMES EVEN MORE DIFFICULT

There are times when the monotony and irksomeness of hospital life make you feel that you want to sit down and scream. I think that I had got to that pitch at that particular moment.

I felt frightful.

Being called at six, going on duty at seven-thirty for twelve long hours. Perhaps there were patches off, a couple of hours in the afternoon, only long enough to parade down through Wigmore Street to catch a glimpse of the park, and then to return again before you could feel freedom.

Like this I never even knew what time of the year it was save by the baskets of flowers that the old women sell in the streets, or by the treetops waving along the Bayswater Road. It wasn't living, it was existing. And every year one gets a little bit older. Every year something more that is precious and worth all else put together slips away from one, and can never be recaptured.

In everybody's life there comes a time when one feels desperate at seeing oneself in a rut from which there is no escape. But I think that it must be almost worse for a trained nurse, because her life is so dreadfully stereotyped.

Patients coming and going; as soon as you grow fond of them they drift off again and out of your life for ever. Finishing for the night with all the flowers set about the corridors, and the night nurses coming on duty. Taking the day report books down to Miss Vaughan, and then trooping off to the basement dining-room to the same dull old suppers.

Always the print frocks and spruce apron,

and the innate longing to get into a gay evening dress, something fussy and frilly, something to make you feel young and gay, part of a glamorous crowd. All that longing pent up inside you until it hurts.

I felt it desperately that night.

It was always such innocuous conversation round that table at night, with Miss Vaughan carving and speaking to each one of us in turn. I felt like a schoolgirl, and it was absurd, because we were all grown women, with our own lives to live, and our own futures, and that future looked like going on and on like this for ever.

'It is the most satisfying job in the world,' said Miss Vaughan from her place at the head of the table. Yet I wondered if she had admitted the truth. Would it not have been more satisfying for her to have been Mrs. Somebody or other, and to have had children? Oh, I know we were all doing good and useful work, mending tired, broken bodies and setting them back on their road to life again, but sometimes there is yourself to think of, and just at that particular moment I was thinking hard of myself.

I had come to a crossways in my life.

I had been shocked by what Tenny had told me, and dreadfully upset by the scene we had had in the little nurses' sitting-room; I had been almost more surprised by the way Ray Harper had talked to me, and by his confession that his marriage was a failure, and that he wanted me to help him with Flower.

Nobody thought about me at all.

In my dilemma I almost thought of pretending to be ill, anything to make my escape.

Of course with the morning I saw sense, and pulled myself together and faced the day properly. It was not any good making mountains out of molehills. The thing to do was still to make an attempt to avoid going away with Flower Harper, and, if the worst came to the worst, admit the truth to him. When the stitches were out it wouldn't matter if she were upset.

And the stitches would be out soon.

When I went on duty with the breakfast in the morning, I found her in quite a different mood. She was gay and perverse and, I thought, determined to tease me.

'You don't like Bill?' she asked me first.

'My opinion doesn't matter.'

'I am quite sure that you think that I am rather a disgraceful sort of person, and that you disapprove of me frightfully.'

She waited for me to say something.

I said, 'It isn't for me to criticize my patients. All sorts and kinds pass through my hands. I don't think about their private lives at all, only about making them well again.'

That didn't satisfy her, and I had had a pretty

good idea that it wouldn't.

'I am sure you would much rather that Bill did not come down to stay at Ventnor.'

Stung by her questions I said that I did think it was a great pity, and personally I would very much rather that I never saw him again.

'I am so afraid that you may try to get out of taking me there,' she said plaintively, 'and it would be awful to go away with a strange nurse. Some of them are too awful, aren't they? I'd hate that. If I promise you that Bill shall not come down there, will that make it better for us both?'

Unfortunately I told her the truth, as I went round her room dusting it. The old maid who has been with Miss Vaughan for years does everything else for us, but the day nurses coming on duty have to dust after her; this always means a chance for the patient to ply us with questions when we have very little opportunity to escape them.

'I have promised Dr. Harper that I will take you away afterwards and I shall not break that promise. I have also told him that I will see after you there, and I will. But it is not part of my job to chaperone you. It will be very much easier for me and for us both if Captain Dawson does not come down there, but it isn't for me to ask you to make promises.'

Again she said, 'He won't be there,' but I knew that she was very angry with me for talking straightly to her, and that quite probably she would get round that promise some way or other.

I finished my dusting and went off to the other patients on the floor. Outside I found that some more flowers had been sent to her, and as I took them from the porter there came the unmistakable scent of hyacinths.

I remembered what Tenny had told me, and instantly my heart missed a beat. I turned aside a corner of the tissue paper covering and saw that they were white hyacinths in a pottery bowl. Could they be from Bill? If he had stuck to his old policy of white violets, why not stick to the same routine with white hyacinths?

I wondered if he had become so scared at meeting Tenny face to face in the nurses' little sitting-room that he had decided to finish the whole thing and not run the risk of meeting any of us again. It would of course be the wisest course of action. Then, just as I was hoping we were through with Captain Dawson, a card dropped out of the flowers, and I saw that it was a woman's visiting card, and knew that I had allowed my imagination to run right away with me, for this was just an ordinary gift, sent quite accidentally by a woman friend.

I took them in.

Flower glanced up.

'Surely you aren't bringing me white hyacinths?' she gasped.

Then I knew! I realized as though she had spoken the words herself that Bill had made a pledge with her as he had done with Tenny, and that the wretched old white hyacinths would be his signal of farewell.

What a man!

'There's a card with them,' I said and handed it stiffly to her. The moment she read it she burst out laughing and then tore it up into little fragments.

'It gave me quite a turn,' she said, 'and all the time they come from poor old Mrs. Pratt. I must be very weak to give myself the jim-jams like that, and all about nothing.'

Within the next two days the specialist came and got the stitches out (what a fuss she made over that too!). It meant that she was well on the way to convalescence. All the arrangements were now set going for us to proceed to the Isle of Wight, and I recognized the fact that there was not to be any escape for me.

I had got to go through with it.

Two days before Flower was to leave the home I went down to Miss Vaughan about it. She was sitting in her private room, where she always saw her nurses; generally it was a case of telling us off about something or other, because although she was very big-hearted and generous, she had definite ideas about duty and the sacrificing of self to the one object.

She told me that she had got everything ready

and had engaged a temporary nurse to take my place. She hoped that I would not think because I was going away for a holiday that I could stop working, as it would be my duty down there as much as up here in the home to see that Mrs. Harper did not overtax her strength.

I stood there listening to her and saying 'Yes, Miss Vaughan' and 'No, Miss Vaughan,' and even as she was talking I wanted to scream. It was so frightful to think that this would be going on all my life, for ever and ever, and much worse when I was an old lady and white-haired like some of the Sisters in the home, that I should still be standing there gauchely like a schoolgirl and saying yes and no.

'You will return in a fortnight, because I cannot spare you for longer than that,' she said. 'I have only engaged the new nurse for that length of time, and you must promise me not to try to extend it, unless there are very urgent reasons for it.'

I promised.

After all I did not think that I should want to make the holiday much longer. It was not going to be very happy for me seeing Flower with her husband in their own intimate private life. I could not imagine now why I had ever been induced to say that I would go. I suppose I had not realized how deeply and desperately I was growing to care for Ray. I ought to have done, because I am not the sort of girl who is easily carried away by men. I can say quite honestly that there has never been anybody else in my life, and I know that there never could be. Which makes it all the worse. I remember my grandmother saying to me once, 'It is hard for you, Dallas, harder than most girls, because if ever you do fall in love, you will fall hard and hurt yourself badly.'

I was falling hard enough.

But then love like that, which lights itself as a torch within you, is an undying flame. It was something which would go on as long as I lived, it would sear its way right through my own heart, and become part of me for ever.

I hadn't been wise to say that I would go away with Flower Harper, but then love is not wise.

'I envy you,' said Tenny, when we discussed it in the nurses' room, though of course she did not know the ins and outs of it all. 'Fancy going away and being with her in some lovely hotel and then having him down for the week-ends! He always makes me feel that he is too good-looking. He ought to have been on the movies and not in medicine at all. I do envy you.'

'I wish that you were going in my place,' and in some ways I did wish it.

Tenny laughed.

'Yes, but you wouldn't say that if it could

really happen. I'd give a lot to be in your shoes, and to have her lovely clothes, even if it were only to handle them, and to meet amusing people and have decent meals for a change and not to be just Nurse.'

'Yes, but what about my uniform?' I asked. 'That will give me away, and I shall be just Nurse.'

Tenny ignored that.

'Being Nurse in a home where there are lots of you, all disgruntled spinsters, and being Nurse in a hotel where you are a rarity, are two very different kettles of fish,' she said.

'Anyway, I don't suppose it will be very gay.'

'It will be a change, and I'd give a lot for a change,' she answered.

## 2

I had been quite wrong about the uniform. Flower mentioned it to me that last evening in the home, when I was seeing her into bed for the night. She said that hotels were fussy and some of them objected to a nurse being about the public rooms, because they thought that it made other inhabitants nervous. Wouldn't it be almost better if I took some plain clothes with me and wore them?

I suppose my face showed by its utter blankness that I hadn't got much that I could take. As a matter of fact I had practically nothing. Nurses don't want a lot of plain clothes, and I had lost interest in them. The chance to wear them appeared so infrequently that I had gradually given up buying them, and at that identical moment, although I could have raked up an old skirt and a couple of blouses and a rather seedy black evening dress, which would do duty for dinner, or smart tea, or a theatre or anything, and nothing really adequately, that was just about the limit of what I could do.

She said that she could make that right for me, if I wouldn't be offended, as she was wildly extravagant over clothes and bought hosts of things that she never wore. We were about the same size too. She explained that she had had the impertinence to order a trunk to be sent to me and I could take what I fancied, and throw the rest away if I liked.

I did not know what to say, and tried to begin expressing my thanks, but words rather failed me.

She had the trunk sent round, and when it appeared next morning insisted that I should choose myself some things out of it. They were marvellous clothes. There was a neat coat and skirt for travelling, with satin blouses. My wretched voile ones would look too shabby for words beside them. There were a couple of semi-evening frocks, and an evening coat.

'You mustn't thank me,' she said, 'it was really Ray's idea. He thought you wouldn't object and that it would make it so much easier for you.'

His idea! It was so like him to think of other people, so like him to be so helpful.

'I don't know what to say,' I stammered.

'Well, keep your thanks for him. Do you know that I believe you are the first woman he has ever noticed since he married me? I ought to be jealous; still, I think I'm safe,' and she laughed.

I knew that I was blushing. I knew that the colour simply rushed to my face, and no wonder. Even if she were right (and of course she wasn't), it was a horrible thought. It was something that I could hardly bear.

I said good-bye to everybody at the home, and they were wild with envy at my luck. A fortnight away, a fortnight without their rice pudding and cold mutton meals, with Miss Vaughan presiding, and the hours spent in the nurses' sitting-room, and the eternal life which went on in its monotonous circle.

I did not see Ray before we left. It was a busy morning, and I heard that he was doing three operations, one here and two up the road at the enormous new nursing home which towers over all the others.

I put on the new coat and skirt which Flower had discarded, and when I looked at myself in the glass in my room, I was a new woman. Clothes make such a enormous difference. I was no longer just a nurse off duty in a reach-me-down serge suit with a voile blouse and a dowdy hat. I was actually smart for the first time in my life. Never before had I seen that there was a possibility behind my plainness. I'd got used to the fact that I was an ugly duckling. You get terribly used to plain looks; the inferiority complex which they breed is something which it is difficult if not impossible to choke down. I had always envied beauty, always been hungry for lovely eyes and a sweet mouth, or a skin like those you see some women possess. They were things that I should never have, I felt. In my family life at home all my relations had thought it amusing to laugh about my plainness. They did not mean to hurt and I don't suppose they ever realized for a single moment that it did hurt me. They just took it for granted that I was plain, and therefore fair game to be teased about it.

Suddenly in that prim little room I saw a new woman look out of the glass at me, a woman with a slick figure, shown off to the best advantage in a suit which was cut on good lines. A woman with poise.

'Oh, it can't be me,' I gasped.

We had an easy train journey and crossed to the Island in the most perfect weather. I had never been there before. In fact I don't think I had ever crossed the sea before, and it seemed to me like going to a foreign country. I would not have dared confess that I felt like this, one has a natural reticence and hates confessing to a childish emotion, but that was the way I did feel. A sea which was pale blue like turquoise, and a sky flecked with little apricot clouds; it was one of the most perfect afternoons that I can remember. When at last we settled ourselves in a ridiculous little train, it was to see the green island stretching on either side, and the downs at Brading, and the sea again at Sandown.

'It's nice,' I said.

Flower glanced out of the window indifferently. 'Oh, it is all right,' she agreed.

She was looking tired, as though she had done too much, and I told her that the moment we got to the hotel she would have to lie down. She had better have her dinner in bed, as if she over-tired herself now it would only retard her convalescence.

'If you are going to be dragon to me, I shall wish you hadn't come,' she said, but I knew that she did not feel too well, because she drooped more and more, and when the train came ultimately to a standstill at Ventnor I think she was quite glad to know that bed was so near.

We went straight up to her room, a large double room looking across the English Channel. As I entered with her leaning on my arm I gave a quick start. There was a faint unmistakable essence which pervaded the place, and I glanced across to the bed. By the side of it was a bowl full of white violets.

'Yes, they came for Mrs. Harper,' said the manageress, who had shown us up. 'They were marked "flowers," and they were likely to die, so that we took the liberty of opening the box and putting them in water. We looked amongst the wrapping but there was no card with them.'

'No card,' she said. 'How odd!'

But it wasn't odd at all. They were the white violets which were to tell her that Captain Dawson himself would be down with us before very long. I might have guessed that she would not keep her promise, she wasn't that sort of woman. Flower had had life run all her own way and she expected it to go on playing into her hands.

I said nothing at all until the manageress had gone, and then as the door closed on her I rounded on Flower.

'You promised me that he wouldn't come down here.'

'Can I help it if he comes? After all this hotel is open to anybody who chooses to book a room at it. It isn't my fault.'

'But you did promise.'

'I'm tired, you can't badger me now. I don't know what is happening, nor what he is doing. I don't understand why the violets are here, I don't care much. Oh, I am so tired, so dreadfully tired.'

In spite of that she insisted that she would come down to dine. I used every argument in my power to try to dissuade her, realizing the foolishness of such a move after the journey, but she looked like working herself up into a fury over it. I knew this would be far worse for her than letting her come down, so I gave way, I am afraid with a bad grace. It was quite obvious to me that she was going to be a very troublesome patient. Although I had chafed against the monotony of the home, and everything that it stood for, the main joy about it was that it was easy there to keep your patients in control. It wasn't so easy when you got them away, and they were determined to get the bit between their teeth.

I did not wear uniform, because she had said she preferred plain clothes in the hotel. I wore the evening frock that she had given me, the one so different from anything I had had before. I sound so vain about all this, but it wasn't vanity which stirred me when I saw myself in new clothes. I was proud to put them on, and proud to go down for the first time in my life not so noticeably labelled 'old maid.'

The moment I got into the room I saw Captain Dawson sitting at a table, and I felt instinctively that he saw me. He was the kind of man who would never miss the sight of a woman. He made me feel actually sick, because

I knew that my hands were tied, and that there was very little I could do. I could, of course, threaten to leave her, but then she was not really strong enough to do without me, and in a sense this would be letting her husband down.

He talked to her, but all the time I felt that his eyes were wandering round to me again. I suppose he could not make head or tail of my being out of uniform, and looking so different. He said nothing. It was horrible, but I kept feeling his eyes on me; it was the knowledge that he looked at me furtively, never so that I could actually see him, but with the appreciation which is not a compliment, and which you feel instinctively.

Afterwards we three had coffee in the lounge.

'So you got the white violets that I sent you,' he said, 'I wasn't very long in following them up, was I?'

'No.'

He turned to me.

'I suppose you like flowers, Nurse, or do you get your fill of arranging them for other people? Have you any favourite ones?'

I seized the opportunity and said, 'Oh, yes, my favourites are white hyacinths,' and I thought he could take it or leave it as he felt best.

He had the grace to blush a little, and I knew that he had got my meaning. Yet he went on glancing at me doubtfully as though he wondered if I knew or had made a lucky shot.

It was most uncomfortable for me sitting there that evening wondering what I ought to do about this. Was a nurse's first duty really to her patient? I did owe Ray Harper something. I did not know what to do, and when the clock struck nine I went upstairs to get the room ready for Flower. She knew that she must be in bed early, and that she was not yet allowed to stay up late, and she had promised me that she would come up in a few minutes.

Of course she didn't.

When I went down to look for her she was not in the lounge where I had left her talking, but I peeped on to the terrace and saw her curled up in a corner, wrapped in a big coat and sitting close to Captain Dawson.

I went to her deliberately, and I admit that I was really very angry.

'Mrs Harper, it is time that you came to bed.'

'I'll be up soon, Nurse.'

'You really must come up now with me,' I insisted.

She was very annoyed at being spoken to like that, and she turned sharply towards me. 'I'm not coming and you must go away. How dare you come here and disturb me?'

I took her arm.

'Now, don't be foolish, I am here to see after you and you have had a tiring journey. You don't realize that you have done more to-day than ever since your operation. You will do yourself harm if you don't come to bed. Please, Mrs. Harper.'

I must give Captain Dawson that much due, for he did see my point and try to help me.

'Yes, Flower, you must do what the little dragon says. Fancy it being such a little dragon!'

She was not going to accept the decree as easily as I had hoped, and she behaved like a naughty spoilt child.

'You are all against me and are being unkind to me. How can you do it?'

However, I insisted, and I got her upstairs. In the lift I had a pretty shrewd idea that she was bottling up a scene for later, and I was only too right. In the big bedroom she rounded on me in a fury, I don't think I have ever seen anyone angrier.

'How dare you? Whatever made you do such a thing? You know as well as I do that you have no right to treat me like a child, and if you think that I am going to put up with it you make a huge mistake.'

I stood my ground.

'I am here, Mrs. Harper, and I hold myself responsible to your husband for your well-being.'

'My husband!'

'What is more, you promised me that Captain Dawson would not be coming down here, and yet I actually find him in the very hotel the moment we arrive. You must admit that it isn't very fair of you.'

'Why shouldn't I have my own friends?'

'Why should you promise me one thing, and then quite deliberately break it?'

She was more indignant than ever over that, and started a tirade. 'How dare you appoint yourself as my keeper? You and my husband have been talking about me behind my back. You think that I don't know about it all, but there you are wrong, because you cannot cheat me as easily as you think.'

I realized all too well how bad a scene of this sort was for her, but although I did my best to calm her, it was quite apparent that she had gone beyond all bounds, and that there was nothing more that I could do. Finally, my patience gave way.

'Look here,' I said, 'I won't be responsible for you any more. I promised Dr. Harper that if anything went wrong I would wire for him, and I shall send the telegram in the morning.'

'You'll get him down here?'

'I certainly shall.'

'You little cat!' That was the first time that she had shown herself in her real colours, but of course in her present temper she hardly knew what she was saying. 'As if I didn't know all along that you were in love with him, and wanted him for yourself! As if I hadn't seen it sticking out a mile, and you supposing that I was blind as a bat all the time! Oh, you think you have been very clever, but you haven't done as well as you think you have. I can promise him that. If you do send for him, I shall tell him that you are in love with him.'

I don't know what I said.

It was a ghastly night and I sat up with her until it was almost dawn, when at last I persuaded her to take a sleeping draught. Later I tiptoed out of the room when she was safely asleep, and I telephoned to the doctor. It was all very well, but I dared not hold myself responsible if she was going to fly into hysterical outbursts of this kind. If she upset herself so violently she would do tremendous harm, and I seemed unable to control her. It would probably mean that she did carry out her threat, and that I went back to London quickly, and it was the end of our friendship, but I don't think I cared. I did not want to stay down here and have Captain Dawson making eyes at me, and all the while knowing that we were hoodwinking her husband. I wanted to get away, and to make the clean break as quickly as I could.

'I'm sorry to disturb you at such a time,' I told him when he came to the telephone, 'it's Nurse Day. Mrs. Harper isn't very well. She got worked up last night, and there has been a frightful scene.'

He asked me tersely for technical details. Her pulse. Her manner. What dose had I given her? I explained that she had had one of her medinals and would be unlikely to wake before midday.

He asked then about Captain Dawson.

'Is that man down there?'

'Yes.'

I'd said it now. I might be a traitor, and what I said might worry him, but it was better to speak the truth than to let the matter drift as it was doing.

'Right, I'll be down about one o'clock. That is the earliest train that I can catch,' and he rang off.

I went back to my patient, who slept heavily on through the morning. She was so fast asleep that I left her to go downstairs for my breakfast, and Captain Dawson was just going out riding. He was at the next table, and he glanced across at me at once. He was a fine-looking man in his riding kit, if you cared for the type, but I hated him. He was so florid and brazen-looking, so horribly, impertinently sure of himself.

'What a little dragon it was!' he kept saying, 'what a little dragon! I wonder if you would be like that to me if I were your patient. Wonder if you wouldn't be a little kinder to a mere man, eh?'

I did not encourage the conversation.

'I'm afraid a nurse very often cannot afford to

be kind.'

'I'm sure that you could be lovely.'

Again those eyes which I knew thought of me only as a woman. They were horrid eyes, and they gave me that nasty squirmy feeling inside which a woman so often gets when a man looks at her in that particular way. He was detestable.

I could not stay there a moment longer than I could help, it was too uncomfortable a breakfast for me, so I got up and went back to Flower. She slept on and on.

The horse came for Captain Dawson, and I watched him ride away and up the side of the hill on his way to St. Boniface Down. He glanced back once and saw me there and waved to me. I was angry with myself that I should have pandered to idle curiosity and had watched him at all.

I tried to forget everything but my patient. Soon the doctor would be down, and even if she did tell him everything that she had promised to tell, it would be a help to know that he was here and to hold him responsible for her. It would be a help to know that he was in the place.

3

It seemed hours waiting for the time when Dr. Harper's train would come in. Presently, half an hour before he was due, Flower started stirring. She woke heavily and slowly.

'Oh, my head, my head,' she said.

I took her the eau-de-Cologne.

'Now don't worry, Mrs. Harper, you are quite all right and here is a cup of tea all ready for you.'

She moaned as she lay there, letting me bathe her forehead with the eau-de-Cologne, and making no attempt to help herself at all.

'Is that you, Nurse?'

'Yes, I'm here.'

'Something happened last night.'

She had her eyes open now, and they were sullen as she lay there staring into space. I went over to the gas-ring and stopped the kettle which was on the verge of boiling over; I made her a cup of tea and brought it to her side.

'Drink this before you attempt to talk. You will find that it makes you feel quite a different woman.'

She tried to push it away.

'I don't want it.'

She was one of the most childish people when she started, and had to be coaxed into drinking it, for all the world like a very little girl.

'Come now, it will do you lots of good, and ease that headache. You want to get rid of that head, don't you?'

I think she lay there trying to recall all the details of the night before, because after a bit she seemed to remember.

'I know. I remember it all now. You came down and made me come up here to bed when I didn't want to do it. You were beastly to me and rude. Oh, I don't know what I couldn't have done to you.'

'You were already over-tired, and had done far too much for one day.'

'Yes, you turned all prim and grand about it. I suppose it is that you don't like Bill being down here, you want him for yourself, I suppose. He is far too good-looking.'

I was very angry at the mere suggestion.

'You mustn't think such things,' I said. 'Captain Dawson is hardly the kind of man that I should ever think twice about. You have no right to say such stupid things even if you *are* angry with me.'

She eyed me over the cup of tea which at last she had consented to drink, though I don't suppose she even tasted it.

'Oh no, of course. You pretend to be so virtuous and so grand about it all, and really it is my husband that you want. A nice thing that is, a very nice thing! You and Ray. Don't make me laugh!'

It seems absurd that one can be so bitterly hurt by people saying things like that. She was quite beside herself with fury, and a sick woman to boot. It is ridiculous that the silly remarks of angry, jealous women like Flower can cut so deeply, but I knew then the meaning of the old proverb which says that words can kill you. I tried to keep my temper. I tried to tell myself that she was ill, and that you could not pay any attention to the things that she said, but all the time it seemed that something inside me was hurt desperately badly, and that I would never forgive her for it.

'I hate you,' she screamed, working herself into a furious passion. 'You care for Ray. You want to get him from me. You know that all the time you are scheming and plotting to get him for yourself. You think I can't see it, think I don't know. Don't be funny! I know that you are in love with him. I know that you despise me because I can't think of him as being anything but a sententious fool. I can't stand his quietness, his reserve, his coldness. He isn't a man, he is a chunk of marble. Go on! Be in love with him! A fat lot of good it will . . .'

Then she stopped short.

I saw her eyes staring at the door behind me and turned intuitively. There, standing staring at us both was Dr. Harper. I don't know how long he had been there, but I do know that he must have heard every word.

Just for a moment she seemed to be paralysed to find that he had heard her, then her eyes goggled and she turned, her mouth sagging.

'Well, I don't care. Now you both know that I know. Go on being in love with each other. I shan't try to stop it. Go on!'

She turned her face to the pillow, sobbing violently. I thought she would hurt herself badly, and I got up to go to her, but my knees seemed to be wobbly and weak; I had little control over myself. That was when Dr. Harper went to the bed.

'That will do, Nurse,' he said.

It was my dismissal.

Well, anyway I could not have stopped on after this horrible scene. I could not have stayed even if I had wanted to. If it hadn't been true, the accusation would not have mattered so much, but it had been true. I *did* love him, and she *had* recognized it.

I went off quietly to my own room and put my things together. It would not take me very long to pack, for my belongings were few. I always travel lightly. The one wisp of an evening frock, a coat and skirt and an afternoon dress. They were all that I had brought with me. I would not accept her clothes, but would leave them behind for her; I must have been mad to have taken them in the first place.

When I had finished I sat there for a little while trying to pull myself together, because this was not too easy. Then I went downstairs into the hall to look up the trains.

I borrowed an A.B.C. from the inquiry office, and was looking in this when the doctor came down the stairs and saw me.

He said, 'Nurse, what are you doing?' and his tone was very sharp. I knew that he was startled. For a moment I did not know whether to try to shuffle out of it with an excuse, or to tell him the truth, which was that I could not bear to stay. Then I decided on the truth.

'I could hardly stay, could I?'

I saw the muscles of his face twitching, and the hurt look in his eyes. It was very seldom that he ever showed what he was feeling, for he wore that mask which every doctor can don to perfection. When he wanted to hide his thoughts he could hide them better than any man I ever met, but this was no time for that kind of thing. He was wretched, and I knew it.

'Isn't there somewhere where we could talk? Somewhere where we should not be disturbed? I have got to have this thing out.'

The hotel book-keeper who had been listening to every word in her little glassed-in desk, peered forward and suggested the card-room, which at this time of the day was always empty. We went inside. It was small and looked desolate and bare, for the card-tables were stacked together in a corner, and the fire had only recently been lit. There was no warmth in it; it flickered with a jaundiced light, but I felt so disturbed and so dreadfully anxious as to what would happen next that I don't think I noticed much. There were two easy chairs before that miserable fire, and I went to one hoping that it would prop me up. My knees wobbled, and I felt really ill.

He came across to the hearthrug and stood

there, his hands sunk into the pockets on either side of his double-breasted coat. It was the way that he always stood. It was a characteristic attitude of his, his eyes watching me, his voice low.

'I want to apologize on my behalf and on Flower's for the dreadful scene that has just been forced upon you upstairs.'

His voice was quite official, and I heard mine replying, very faint and very far away. I was saying something foolish about it being all right, when all the while I knew that it was not all right. It was one of the most horrible scenes I had ever been through.

'I told you when you undertook this case that my wife was a very difficult patient. I did not think that she would behave like this, because I hoped that she had got over her habit of making scenes. She hadn't! I told you before you came down here that our life together had been complicated and difficult.' It seemed now that all the doctor's mask of reserve had slipped and I was looking into the heart of the man, the real man, who had suffered terribly.

'Please don't tell me,' I begged.

'A man hates to admit failure, but I have failed. The thing that hurts me now is that the fact of my own failure should hurt others. For instance, a girl like yourself, who had been subjected to one of these very painful scenes.'

'I shall forget it,' I said, and realizing how

miserable he was, pulled myself together and tried to reassure him. 'This sort of thing comes all in the day's work, and it is nothing to worry about.'

Still there was something that he was keeping back, which I realized, for he still stood on, his brows knit, his hands still sunk deeply.

'Please,' he said, 'do not suppose for a single moment that I shall ever remember what she said. In medicine the best and kindest thing to do is to forget. I know that her remarks were quite wrong.'

'She jumped at some foolish conclusions,' I reminded him, 'but then she is a sick woman, and sick people do get silly fancies.'

But the conclusions, unfortunately, had been right. I did love him, and knowing how much he was going through I could only love him more, not as a doctor, but as a man—the man with the wounded heart which he was showing me for the first time.

'It is all terrible,' he said, as though he had arrived almost at breaking point. Then quickly, because I think he realized that he wanted to get it over, 'I have always had a very sincere admiration for you; she knows that, and that is why she has said these insane things. She can't help it, and you must forgive her. Flower has all her life been inordinately jealous.'

'Please don't speak of it. It is quite all right. I know that she did not mean what she was saying.'

He stopped speaking.

I saw him looking at me, and in his eyes was something to which I could not blind myself. It was not imagination. It was not the longing in my own self which had provoked this look; it was the fact that at that particular moment I realized that he cared for me—she had been quite right. It showed in every line of his face, in every expression, and it was going to make my future a great deal more difficult.

Perhaps I should have controlled myself, but I couldn't. The tears were coming, and I knew that I had got to get out of the room, and quickly, or break down, which would be awful.

I said before I could stop myself: 'It has been so dreadful! Please, I just can't go on nursing her; I can't bring myself to go through with it. Do let me go back to the home. Nothing can ever make this position possible, and we have to think of her.' Then I was ashamed that I had said so much.

He took my hand and gripped it hard. We may have stood there for a minute or an hour. I don't know which it was. I don't suppose I cared.

When he spoke again his voice was quite ordinary and calm, just as though the whole thing had never happened at all, and we were doctor and nurse discussing a troublesome patient who had given us more than the usual amount of trouble.

'Of course I understand. I know exactly what you mean. You could not go on nursing her under these conditions, and it would be too much to ask of you. I will telephone Miss Vaughan that you are on the way back, and will explain that it is no fault of yours.'

'Thank you.'

I wanted to linger, even though the lingering hurt me a good deal more. But he had greater sense than I had, for he went to the door and held it open for me.

I think that I shall always remember the little card-room, and can see it again to-day. A crowd of tables stacked in the corner, the newly-lit fire wheezing among the sticks, and the way that Ray had looked at me there, his eyes telling me the truth about his feelings for me.

'Good-bye, Dallas.'

I went back upstairs and put on my bonnet and cloak, feeling almost numbed. The porter had already fetched down my luggage. It was going to be dreadful returning to the home which I had left only such a few hours before. Everybody would be asking questions. It would take something to put Tenny off, and that Night Sister Johnson who had been jealous of my getting the trip at all.

Still, I hadn't got back to the home yet, I kept telling myself, sufficient to the day is the evil thereof.

I went out of the hotel and drove away.

## 4

It was bound to be a wretched journey up to London. I kept telling myself that I must pull up my socks and have some sort of a story ready; in the home Dr. Harper was a hero, and everybody hung round him and every word that he uttered, so that they would be all agog to know what could have happened to explain my speedy return from nursing his wife.

It wasn't going to end here.

It was going to be dreadfully difficult meeting him again when he came in to operate. It would be far better if I were never to see him again, and yet instantly I knew that life without him would be unthinkable. I could not let the whole affair drop, even though it might be fairer to his wife, and to me in the long run. It would be quite dreadful seeing him only across the operating theatre, his face masked, the stern, cold, resolute man who was fighting for his patient's life. His orders being rapped out authoritatively, and all the while the sounds of the operating theatre, the tenseness, the tinkle of an instrument being flung into an enamel bowl, and he giving me orders and directions, inquiring as to symptoms and no more.

Now there would never be the chance for us to meet again in any friendly or intimate circumstances. They had all been put behind me.

Tenny would know!

And Birdie and Sister Johnson would know. The whole home, surging round the incident, would make the most of it, and their questions and conjectures and gay banter were all going to hurt me dreadfully.

Only I had got to go back to them.

The train seemed to race too fast, or to go too slowly; I did not know which. Eventually it drew into Waterloo Station, with the crowds surging round it, and never a friendly face among them all. There is nothing much more lonely than a big London station when you come to think of it, and here some of the most tragic farewells and meetings, and some of the happiest ones, are staged.

I saw lovers walking hand in hand, and envied them. I saw lovers parting, and even envied them those brief tears. All my life I had wanted to fall in love, and had set it high above me as being the most exquisite experience that life could give me, now I knew that it was a cruel experience and that it hurt more than all others and would go on hurting for the rest of my life. Because there was no way out.

The taxi took me to the home. We drove into that district which seems to be entirely peopled by the medically minded—Harley Street, Wimpole Street, Welbeck Street, with all their little offshoots of nursing homes and hospitals.

They were long, silent streets where, behind shuttered windows, doctors give verdicts, terrible verdicts, or those which released sufferers from pain. I saw visions of white caps fluttering behind those uncurtained windows. How well I know it all, and my whole life would be spent here!

The taxi stopped at the home itself, and I got out and rang for George to help with my luggage.

I knew now, perhaps for the first time, how new patients must feel when they arrive for their operation, because I felt exactly like it. The shivering on the brink. That awful expectancy of something dreadful and unknown which lay ahead. An operation on the senses, which was what was happening to me!

I had come back to forget that there was such a man in the world as Ray Harper, even though his eyes had admitted the truth, and he had confessed that he cared for me; even though we both loved one another, I had got to put all that behind me.

I had come into the home to get well from that almost incurable malady of the heart—the malady of being in love.

Miserably I went inside.

Miss Vaughan greeted me in her sitting-room, and I felt again like a naughty schoolgirl.

She expressed surprise. Oh, yes, she had

talked to the doctor on the telephone this morning, but she was most surprised to think that I had come back so soon. It didn't do for nurses to quarrel with their patients. She seldom let a nurse take a patient away, and now she much regretted that she had done it in this case.

I knew that she was angry.

It upset all her arrangements, of course, and she had got the temporary nurse in doing my work. I should have to go back to the theatre for to-day while she made arrangements. Back to pro's work. Back to swabs and enamel bowls, and clearing up and sterilizing. Back to the dirty jobs.

The odd thing was that none of the others said a word; they seemed to accept my return all calmly as though it were quite the usual thing to happen.

'Oh, so you've come back.'

'What's Ventnor like?'

'Did you have a nice time? How is she getting on?'

I had got to take up life again and realize that all that had happened had been a passing affair, something gone for ever now. I had to absorb myself in the routine which would go on for the rest of my life, something which was inescapably part of me. It would surround me.

On duty at half-past seven every morning of my life, trooping up the stairs after the chilly breakfast in the basement, with the discussion of the night report books and the same old chatter of the nurses who never went anywhere or saw anything beyond the four walls of the home itself. Coming to work and being on duty practically all day, preparing people for the theatre, calming their fears, and then receiving them back again ready to nurse them to health. Taking in bunches of flowers on their behalf and fixing them into vases. Ushering visitors into quiet bedrooms and watching doctors coming and going and Sister superintending.

I sat down in that tiny room of my own, and I thought however should I face it all, how should I manage to go through with it?

Something inside me told me that I had got to.

You can't be cowardly when it comes to living life. I had always longed for romance. What woman doesn't? I had always thought about the marvellous time when a girl fell in love. Well, I had had romance, and I had fallen in love, and I had not gained too much by either of them.

Other women have fallen in love with married men, and they also have suffered for it. Their hearts may have been broken, but they have carried on with the duties which life ordains for them. They have been resolute because they have had to be.

Next morning I was on duty again.

Same old routine. Same old monotony.

'You look awfully pale, Dallas. Not feeling too well?' asked Tenny. Even she had not asked about why I had returned to the fold, and considering that she was usually a very curious person, it was a wonder.

'I don't feel too good.'

'It was that wretched patient of yours. She knocked spots off you. What an exacting woman! I can't think why a beautiful man like Dr. Harper could ever have married her.'

I thought to myself, oh, if he had never married her! But that wasn't going to do either of us much good now. He had spoilt his life, because he had seen a pretty face on the stage, and it was too late to undo what had been done.

We can't go back in life.

Tenny went on talking.

'You've heard about Birdie?' she asked. 'Oh, it was the biggest excitement and it all happened the other night. The Padre in number seventeen fell for her. She just laughs and won't tell us anything about it, but there is more in this than meets the eye. You'll see. Imagine Birdie as a parson's wife! I can't, can you?'

'I can't,' I said.

I didn't want to discuss Birdie's future; I was in that dreadful sore mood when somebody else's happiness hurt a little too much. Perhaps it was selfish, but when you have had a bad blow, you get a reaction. I had got it badly at this moment, too badly. I felt that I wanted to die.

Tenny came closer. She said: 'You're feeling unhappy, I know that. Miss Vaughan called us up and said that there was to be no discussion. She put on her best seven-years-a-matron appearance and that is why nobody has mentioned it, but I wondered if there wasn't anything you'd like to tell me?'

I shook my head.

'There are times when you can't talk about things, Tenny, they hurt too much,' and I turned from her.

If I had stayed I should have made a fool of myself. It would be awful to break down when all my impulse was to go hard and to brazen the whole thing out. Work was obviously the antidote. Work was what I ought to undertake, and that was why I went straight down to the theatre.

Two days later I was put back on the floor again with a case that had just come in.

'It is better for you than theatre work,' said Miss Vaughan, and I was glad to be released, because I had kept thinking all the time how awful it would be if I had to work for *him*. I was just at that pitch when I don't think I could have borne seeing him standing there, authoritative and austere, a man in white who was aloof and who had no time for anyone or anything but the business in hand.

I went to see after the little girl who had come in to have her tonsils removed. She was a bright little thing, watching me with shining eyes.

'Theatre case at eleven,' Sister told me, 'all that is needed is just to keep her amused. She is a bit highly-strung, got a nervy mother, and she needs quietening a little.'

She was a nice little kiddie with bright golden curls and dancing eyes. She was brave too, in spite of what Sister had said.

'They put you to sleep, don't they, so that it shan't hurt you?' she asked.

I knew that she would have an injection and only when that had taken effect would she be given her anæsthetic, but I pretended that she would be taken down to the theatre because she thought that it was the kind of place where they had pantomimes. She had been to see 'The Sleeping Beauty' last year, and was hoping that she would see something of the kind while her tonsils were being taken out.

'It's all like fairies, isn't it?' she asked.

Most patients are scared stiff, although they try to keep it from you, so that her naïve way of putting it made a great change for me.

I explained that only certain people could have their tonsils out and that it made them strong and big and beautiful. She thought it was all great fun.

At half-past ten I suggested that she should get a little nap first, so that she should be all fit and well when she woke up.

'Got to pop something into your arm,' I told her, 'it's all part of the magic, only the fairies get frightened that there might be one wicked one about, and if we put this stuff into your arm it helps them an awful lot.'

She laughed at that. She was awfully good about it too, buttoning up her mouth and then saying, 'I'm glad that's over, it pricks, I s'pects it is because it is such a very bad fairy.'

'That's it,' I told her. 'Now, what about a tiny bit of a snooze and I'll wake you when it is the right time?'

She curled up contentedly enough and presently I saw her eyelids drooping. Sitting beside her, I knew that I envied her mother. It must be a joy to have children and I sometimes wonder if anybody's life is wholly complete without them? If Flower and Ray had had a child of their own I don't believe that they would have been up against such tragic difficulties. I don't believe that they would have drifted so apart and that she would have needed people like Bill Dawson to amuse her. Flower and Ray. There I was thinking of them again when I had promised myself that I wouldn't think of them whatever happened.

I dismissed them quickly out of my mind, and turned again to the child, now sound asleep. That was when I got on the telephone to the anæsthetist in the theatre.

'The patient is unconscious.'

He said: 'Shall I bring her down?'

But she was such a little thing!

'I can carry her quite easily myself,' I said, and rolled her into the blanket. She never stirred as I carried her down, and the fairy magic was there, for I laid her on the theatre table and almost instantly the mask was over her face. She breathed evenly and tranquilly, she would never know anything at all about this.

I hate tonsil ops.

Standing there while they busied themselves about her, I thought that I hated all ops. They would always remind me of him, and I did not want to be reminded of him any more. Wild and idiotic plans seemed to pour into my mind. It would be the easiest thing to go away; to get a job somewhere else, abroad perhaps, somewhere where I would meet fresh people in fresh surroundings and forget all about what I had suffered.

Abroad there are so many more opportunities. Abroad even quite plain people like I was get the chance to meet men, and to marry.

I sounded like a husband-hunter. It wasn't that. I wish words were not such difficult things and that I could explain myself properly, but there is a hunger in life, a distrust of the loneliness which the future offers, a burning desire to leave all that behind and to have someone, even anyone, to share your thoughts and your dreams, your hopes and desires.

It is the loneliness of life which hurts so much; it is the fact that there is no one to stand by your side, no one to care what happens to you, and I am quite sure this is the force which drives a great many women into a marriage when they are not quite sure of their affections.

I saw that the operation was ending, and slipped out of the theatre upstairs to get the room ready for her. On the stairs there were visitors coming and going, people with large bunches of flowers (more work for some nurse, though of course they never looked at it that way), porters with trays. I could hear the sound of Miss Vaughan's voice as she talked to some visitor. 'Well!' I thought, 'thank heavens I can't hear *his* voice for a little while. He will have to stay at Ventnor for a day or two to settle things up there.'

I went on to the room.

Tenny had popped in to see what I was doing. 'Not got her back again yet?'

'No.'

'Nothing wrong?'

'No, perfectly straightforward,' and I suppose she knew by my tone that I wasn't thinking what she said.

Tenny turned to me. 'Men make me sick,' she said quickly, 'I told you that they wouldn't do you any good, Dallas, I warned you that this would happen.'

'You cannot help your own feelings.'

She shook her head. 'No, I couldn't help mine. I suppose if I had had the sense to run away from things it would have been better, if only I had not let them go so far. But the snag is that you never realize how much you are falling in love until it actually happens. White hyacinths.' And she stood there biting her lip as though the memory still had the power to hurt.

'It's over now,' I said.

'Yes, and what is more, something is dead inside me. I'll never love anyone else. I can't. You probably don't understand, but something inside me was killed then. He did that. I'd never care for anybody in the same way again.'

I hadn't meant to let Tenny in on my own private thoughts, but somehow or other it slipped out. I said: 'In the theatre just now I was wondering if it wouldn't be possible for me to get a job right away, abroad somewhere. They are always wanting nurses for outposts of empire, and I don't see why we shouldn't go together.'

'Together?'

'Tenny, we've both suffered a bit, you more than I have. It wouldn't be a bad idea if we pulled up our socks and left everything that can remind us of what has happened and went right away?'

'It would be a wonderful idea if only we could do it.'

I heard the sound of the porters bringing the ambulance stretcher out of the lift, and knew that it was my little patient returning. It was the little girl all right, and I had her room ready and warm so that we popped her straight into bed; almost at once she went off into a sound natural sleep. This might last for some hours, as we knew, and the longer the better, because it would give the throat the chance to start healing. I took my place beside her, hardly stirring.

Her mother came in to see her. I could hear her outside on the landing, and knew that Tenny was trying to explain the situation to her. She wanted to be in and to see how the child was. Yet if she came in the chances were that she would make a fuss and waken the child and harm her.

'You're hurting her,' she kept saying in an agony, 'I know that she wants me and yet you won't let me go to her. I would never have allowed her to come here had I thought that you were going to be so cruel to us both.'

I felt terribly sorry for her, but she might have trusted us.

Nurses don't hurt people if they can help it. We want our patients to get well and to be happy. The longer this little girl could lie there asleep, the less chance of sickness there was for her. And we wanted to guard against that at all costs. But still the mother argued outside the door. It was her argument, and the noise she made, that disturbed the child, so that she moved and began to wake.

I was furious. It is all very well, but the people who retard their dear ones' recovery the most are the relations.

It was nursing that little girl back to health again that made me forget my own troubles somewhat. I knew that she would go out within the week, and I concentrated on getting her fit and well. But life wasn't good.

During that week I wrote to the different Agents for the Colonies and I got papers as to the chances of nursing abroad. I pored over these in my own room, and ultimately I passed the likely ones on to Tenny to have a look at. The world seemed suddenly to have become a much bigger place with prospects all over it. Yet it takes a courageous heart to cut the traces and to start afresh in a new country. I don't believe that I had ever realized how closely one clings to habit, to the flora and fauna that one knows and loves, to the silly little things like wet days, and April skies, like dahlias in autumn, and the leaves turning gold, and the scent of clover in a hay meadow.

I had got to think this over very carefully before I made a definite move.

# 5

I had been telling myself all through this week, if only it could be some little time before I had to meet Ray Harper again, it would be so much easier. If only life would be good to me and give me the chance to conquer myself and keep that stiff upper lip, then I'd be all right.

Life wasn't good!

I was told the very day that the little girl went out of the home with a promise of a lovely holiday at the seaside, that the room was wanted for another patient. Miss Vaughan sent me up the papers with all the particulars written on it. She was a youngish woman with a particularly bad appendix. In the corner, under the single printed word 'Doctor,' I saw his name. I knew then that it was one of his cases coming in for me to nurse. We should be meeting every day for a while; we should be thrown together. It was almost more than anyone could bear.

I must have felt it bitterly, because I pulled myself together and went to see Miss Vaughan about it.

'Can't this patient have another room? Can't somebody else nurse her?' I asked

I knew that my own wound was not yet healed, and seeing Ray would rip it right open again. It sounds melodramatic to say that in some strange way I could feel my heart bleeding, but that was what it seemed to be like. The idea actually hurt me, it hurt horribly.

'Really, Nurse,' said Miss Vaughan. It was one of her bad days, when she had had everything go wrong, and I knew by the way that she tapped on her desk with the pencil that she thought I was worrying her.

'I wouldn't ask you, Miss Vaughan, were it not for the fact that I should find it so impossible.'

I oughtn't to have risked that. Miss Vaughan was one of those people who could never understand how it was that anyone was not prepared to sacrifice her whole life to nursing. She had done this herself. She had given up everything else, and was now absorbed only in her work.

She said: 'Your fault is that you allow personal feelings to interfere with your public duty. If I had wanted anyone else to nurse this patient I should have said so. I have appointed you, and I cannot have all my arrangements upset just because you have some private feeling that you do not care to work for Dr. Harper.'

So she had recognized my motive.

I felt myself colouring, and was annoyed that she should have been so far seeing and should have realized the reason why I did not want to carry on. I was very sorry that I had ever gone down to her sitting-room and had laid my case before her. She wasn't understanding. It was strange, because nobody could be more sympathetic with a patient, but she just had no idea of how the nurses could feel.

Birdie met me on the stairs. Birdie had just got herself into plain clothes ready to go out for her walk after night duty.

'Lovely morning,' said she, 'the birds are singing as though the spring was far advanced; it is all perfect.'

It was plain to see that Birdie was in love, she and the Padre were a very happy couple. I couldn't feel that same way. 'Been in to see Miss Vaughan,' I told her, 'I don't believe she has got a heart. She has never felt like you feel, that's a certainty.'

'Oh, she's all right. She seems a bit prim but she's a darling really,' and off went Birdie humming to herself.

I stood in the hall staring after her. I thought to myself, 'Yes, my girl, you've got it pretty badly if you can feel that way for Miss Vaughan.' Birdie going all romantic. Birdie listening to bird song, and feeling that it was spring. I would never have thought it of her.

When a nurse on night duty goes glamorous, then she very obviously must be in love. There can be no other explanation for it.

That very evening my new patient came in for her operation. She was too ill to walk up the stairs, or to stand in the lift, and the porters brought her up to her room on a stretcher. I knew when I saw her that she was not afraid; it was just that she was in so much pain that she did not care what happened to her. Pain can make you blind to everything else that goes on around you.

She did not come in until just as the night nurses were going on duty, for which I was very thankful. Birdie had her for the night, which meant that I did not see the anæsthetist or the surgeon when they called, and that was one mercy.

When I came on duty first thing in the morning Birdie told me that she had had a bad night, and she had been to and fro with her trying to ease the pain until the small hours when she had slept a little.

I took charge of her.

I was with her when the anæsthetist gave her her first dose in bed.

'Just something in your arm,' he told her, 'and you will get a lovely feeling of sleep.'

She said whitely, 'I feel awful.'

'You'll be feeling fine in a moment.'

He knelt there beside her, making a tourniquet, and I held the things for him. She winced as the needle went in, but almost instantly said, 'Oh, that's lovely. So comfy,' and her head lolled. That particular drug does its work quickly. He looked at her as she went off.

'Poor little kid, that is a pretty sickening pain. Thank heaven she has got some relief now.'

'I'll tell the stretcher men to come in.'

'Oh, no; she weighs nothing. I can carry her in myself.' He stooped over her and rolled her into the blanket.

'There won't be any need for me to come down to the theatre, doctor?' I asked.

'The surgeon asked for you to be there. He said that the nurse in charge of the case must be present.'

'Very well, doctor.'

How can you argue when it is a matter of moments, and the patient is lying there unconscious between you? You can't.

He lifted her into his arms, and I held the door open for him. He walked out and through the big swing doors of the theatre. Ahead of me I saw them waiting. Sister by the instruments, an impassive figure which might have been carved out of marble. The theatre nurse hovering in the background. Miss Vaughan, who never missed any operation, but insisted on always being present. I saw the anæsthetist's bottles and cylinders all grouped together at the head of the table, and then quite suddenly I saw Ray.

I suppose that I shall always remember him as he was then, though I had seen him like it dozens of times before. But that picture is cut into my memory. A man in white with a mask cutting his face off, so that you could only see the eyes watching. He had been waiting for me to come in; he had known when he said 'the nurse in charge of the case' that I should be the girl who would come through those doors. For a moment he had forgotten the theatre and the nurses waiting, and the little patient being laid on the table in readiness for him. I knew that he had forgotten everything but me.

There was no time to waste.

The anæsthetist settled himself at the head of the table, and instantly everything seemed to click to attention. There was the purr of oxygen from a cylinder, the faint smell of anæsthetic, and Ray waiting.

The word of command came.

'She's deeply under now,' from the anæsthetist.

Instantly Ray had whipped off the dressings and exposed the skin which I had painted with iodine in readiness for him. It shone out in a vivid yellow blob under those big lights. He worked rapidly. Standing opposite to them, I could hear the commands he rapped out to the Sister standing by his side.

'The scalpel.'

A moment later he flung them back into the enamel bowl held out by the nurse. Again another command.

'Forceps.'

He was a strange white man, only his hands and eyes showing any sign of life, and the hands in those shining rubber gloves looking peculiarly unreal.

From the head of the table there came a warning:

'Her pulse is dropping. Be quick.'

There was a grunt, his only indication that he had heard. All the effort he could spare himself to make, because his work needed every atom of himself. On and on he went, snipping, putting into place, working, working frantically against time.

'She's stopping breathing,' from the head of the table.

No panic.

I saw Miss Vaughan step forward and take hold of the oxygen cylinder in readiness. There was a tenseness about the air, something vital which throbbed right through us. I felt as though somebody had nailed my feet to the floor; there was that faint gasping of the patient, growing weaker, with longer gaps in between, just that ebbing which might mean disaster.

'Ah,' from the anæsthetist.

From Ray, 'I'm going on. It is her only chance, and if ever she does come round it will be done.' He went on working on a woman who was apparently dead. Somehow I knew that he would not let her go. He is so full of life himself, I thought; he will pass some of that life of his on to her. He would *make* her live.

He drew back.

'All done.'

They were bending over her at the head of the table, injecting something. Then I heard a gasp again. It was the faintly rattling breathing which began like the creaking of a wheezy door. Instantly Ray was stitching her up and bandaging her; the operation was over.

I heard the oxygen spitting as it issued from the cylinder; I saw no panic, but merely the controlled movements of people used to dealing with matters of life and death.

'Swab, please, Nurse,' from Ray.

I hardly realized that he was speaking to me.

The patient was breathing again in little whining breaths, but it was like the sweetest music. I felt myself turning giddy with relief. There was a sound in my own ears, a light burring sound; my head was spinning round me. It was years since I fainted in the theatre, and I thought that I had grown far too proficient for such a thing ever to happen again, but I believed that suddenly I was going to do it in spite of myself.

Then I heard his voice, and it was very angry.

'Swab, Nurse. What are you dreaming about? Pull yourself together.'

It was a hard voice, and the very sharpness of it was what saved me from making a complete fool of myself. I handed him the swab across her body and watched him fix it into place. He made no comment.

'Stretcher,' from the anæsthetist.

Sister pressed the bell and the doors swung open, the pleasantly cool outside air flowing in. The whole thing was over and I knew that she would live. But how he had gone on with his operation without flinching I did not know. Then his voice came, and he was speaking to me, 'Pull yourself together.' I had never thought that he could speak like that, least of all to me.

As I went upstairs with my patient I knew that I felt desperately disappointed in him.

'I'm mad,' I told myself; 'mad to think of him in this way. He doesn't care for me. You can't go on what eyes say; it is the lips that matter most of all.'

I followed my patient into her room.

## 6

I knew that this would be a long and tedious coming round as I took a seat beside her. There was nothing that I could do for her as yet, nothing that anyone could do. She lay there comfortably enough. I hoped that she would not regain consciousness for some time, but would pass into a natural sleep, which is always the best way out of such an emergency.

For a long while she lay there like a log, never stirring, then she made a faint moaning sound, but was still quite unconscious.

Tenny peeped in.

'The husband is here. Can he see her?'

I shook my head. 'She isn't conscious yet, and it would only worry him; he would think that she was in pain.'

'He seems dreadfully upset.'

'He would be more upset if he saw her, and really she is doing splendidly, though he probably would not think that.'

Tenny tiptoed off again.

I sat on very quietly indeed, and it was a whole hour later when I noticed something strange about her face, something different. I turned back the bed-clothes hurriedly and saw a crimson stain on the bandages that Ray had put into place so carefully. Instantly I called for another nurse.

'Ring up the surgeon.'

I got ice for her. She was quite unconscious, and Sister came in to help me. We worked hard from the beginning, but I realized that this was going to be a difficult case. As we worked I heard the door behind me open, and knew without having to look that he was there.

He came across to the bed, and he got down to the dressings. I have been working for doctors most of my life, but it certainly seems that I have never seen a man work as he can. Ray Harper refused to allow his patients to die if he could possibly help it.

'She has got to live,' he kept saying between his teeth.

He took great chances, but with him they were not so great, because he knew that his sheer magnetic personality would pull a patient through. He had that bleeding under control inside a couple of minutes, then he did the bandaging himself.

'I'm staying here,' he said resolutely.

'Staying?'

'Yes. I'm staying until she is round. We can't risk this again, and if it does happen it may be fatal. I've got to be here on the spot.'

He waved Sister aside and took a chair at the head of the bed. I don't think he even realized that I was there. He was oblivious to everything save his patient.

Sister said, 'Very well,' and went out of the room. We were alone. He took no notice of me whatsoever, but sat there much like pictures I had seen of trappers sitting in the middle of the Canadian Rockies, without moving a hair, just watching the movements of a particular animal. He never took his eyes off her face, nor his fingers from her pulse. He did not care what went on around him, because he was concentrating solely on her.

I sat down opposite. There we sat, intensely still, with only the light fluttering of her breathing, only the little gasps every now and then.

At last I think he became vaguely aware of my presence.

He said, 'This has been a tough case.'

'Yes.'

'She'll be all right. I thought she had gone on the table, but she is rounding the corner all right. That hæmorrhage, I don't think it will come again.'

I said 'No' like an automaton.

He was not wholly satisfied even then, as I knew, but a quarter of an hour later he released his hold on her wrist, which I realized showed that he felt better about her.

He got up. Then he looked at me, almost as though he were seeing me for the first time.

'I am afraid that you thought I was unkind when I spoke to you in the theatre. If I hadn't snapped just when I did you would have fainted.'

'I know.'

'We couldn't have that happening to add to all our other troubles. It was one of my most difficult moments; I thought we had lost her.'

'Will she live now?'

'I think so.'

I felt that I had got to talk about the patient, because concentrating on ourselves was far too dangerous a subject, but apparently he did not feel quite the same way.

'I hope you are not angry with me,' and his voice was pathetically pleading. I met his eyes; they were the eyes of a little boy who thinks that he is not going to be forgiven.

'Of course not,' I said.

'I am a very unhappy man,' and his voice was so low that I could hardly hear his words.

There wasn't any time to answer. At that very moment the patient's eyes had flickered open quite unexpectedly, and I knew that she was looking fully into my face. She gave a tiny, brave smile.

'You're back in bed,' I told her; 'it is quite all right, and you are splendid, only you mustn't try to move. Promise me that you won't move.'

I had become all nurse again.

'If you'll hold my hand.'

I put my hand in hers, and so we sat on, hand in hand, with the seconds ticking by. In a moment or two I knew by her deep breathing that she was sound asleep and that it was the natural sleep which would restore her more than anything else in the world.

He glanced at me.

'You're fine,' he said.

He wasn't a doctor any more. He was just a man, and I knew by the way that he spoke that he cared. Gently I released my hand from that of my patient, and as I did so his touched mine. For one second we remained like that, and I felt his fingers gripping mine so that they almost hurt me. I felt all the tenseness, all the pain, and the emotion which he had been experiencing through these few days.

We stood there probably only for a minute,

but there are moments in your life when time stands still. It was like an eternity.

Then he said, 'Forgive me,' and turned quickly, hurrying away from the room.

## CHAPTER FOUR

# THE ROUTINE GOES ON

After that we had to meet as strangers, normally and naturally, just as though neither of us knew that the other one cared.

I cannot begin to explain how hard all that was, or what a strain. It was dreadful to be constantly seeing him whom you adored, with other people always round you. To be constantly talking of unimportant general subjects when in your heart was the burning vital subject that hurt so badly.

I wanted to ask him what was happening to Flower. Had he settled the affair with Captain Dawson, or was that wretched man still hanging round their home? I wanted to ask all sorts of questions, but of course I never got the chance to put one to him.

He cared for me, I knew that, but whether it was the feeling that I had for him I could not tell, and, anyway, I had no right to that feeling, because he and I were in two different types of life, and he was a married man.

I lay awake in bed at night trying to reason this thing out. What was the end of it? There were, of course, the papers which I had got from the Crown Agent people, and which I kept in a little pile. Tenny was all for going on with it. She wanted to get away from the monotony and the routine, but I knew that when it came to the actual break I should be sure to fail her. I had not got the courage to go right away and never to meet him again or see him again. It was absurd, because I knew that I was resenting the fact that we had to meet and speak, because it made me feel so dreadful, but I could not end that dreadfulness.

'You're growing thin, Nurse,' Miss Vaughan announced to me one day in the middle of our cold mutton meal.

'I was too fat before,' I told her.

I think she guessed a little, for she is a very discerning woman. But she said nothing. She just smiled.

Birdie announced her engagement with a half-hoop of sapphires, and Tenny went on with her work. Routine had got us all again and there was no escape from it.

People think that a nurse's life is full of change and enchantment and thrill, but that isn't so. You change one patient for another, one disease for another, but it is no more than that. You do not meet exciting people, for when they come to us they are generally weary, and sick, and crotchety. They are never at their best. When they become at their best again, then they go away.

Occasionally through that dark patch I would see Ray operating, see that masterful being standing over the table, compelling his patients to live. Or I would meet him across somebody's bed, when I was only the nurse. That hurt. I hate being just Nurse and never Dallas.

'This will go on for ever and ever,' I told myself frantically, 'and I can't face it. I just can't go through with it.'

Although it seemed that nothing I could do would change it.

Life was carrying me along on its tide and bearing me away with it. I'd grow old at the nursing home as some of the nurses had done before me. I saw them quite often, and they always reminded me of what lay ahead for me also. Nothing. Just nothing at all.

I don't remember now how long that period lasted. To-day it seems like a bad dream and I can hardly believe that it ever happened, yet during it all I used to watch for Ray, and watch the days come and go, and wonder how on earth I could make a change in them.

The change came on its own.

## 2

One night Ray came in to see a patient of his whom I was nursing. He was awfully pleased with her, and she was going home the next day; he had come in to bid her good night. He said the same to me, and then slipped off downstairs. I busied myself with her, and then, having finished, drew off my cuffs. The long day had ended. The night nurses would be coming on duty, and I got ready to make off down the stairs.

I found Ray at the second bend.

Apparently I was the first person who had come down since he had left me, and he had fallen there in a heap. I knew at once that he must have fainted. I knelt down and loosened his collar. I took his head into my arms, and I am afraid I felt almost glad to have the chance of holding him like that. How I had always longed to touch him, to stroke that thick dark hair. Yet now, when for a moment I held him gently, I was afraid for him because I knew that he was in danger.

I laid him back as comfortably as I could, opened his collar, and felt for his pulse.

The dark eyes opened, and I saw that he recognized me.

'You, Dallas?' he whispered.

'I'm here.'

'Don't let me go. Don't let me go again,' he begged just like a child.

'Of course not.'
'I fainted?'
But I had had my fingers on his pulse and knew that it was not quite that. I heard the rustle of a starched skirt passing by, and still holding him in my arms, called for help. It was Tenny who came down the stairs, coming off duty.
'Get Miss Vaughan,' I told her.
She stared at me and then at him.
'My goodness!' she said.
I don't think it even occurred to me that we must have looked strange, because I was so anxious about him, so worried that he was going to be really ill. Of course the moment Miss Vaughan arrived everything had to be niched and orderly. Luckily the room behind us was vacant, as a patient had just gone out. The porters carried Ray into it and laid him on the bed, and Miss Vaughan sent for the consulting physician, who usually treats people in the home.
'You had better go down to your dinner, Nurse,' she said. 'You came off duty at seven-thirty.'
It was now eight.
'Can't I stay?' I asked.
'Certainly not. You won't be fit to see after your own patients in the morning. Now run along with you.'
I could think of no excuse, so I began,

perhaps rather foolishly, 'You see, having nursed his wife, I know more about him than the others, and I think that he would want me to be here.'

But I saw her eyes and knew that I had got to go.

I was indignant about it, because I knew that he was ill. I had not been a nurse for so long without recognizing danger when I met it, but I had to leave him. I went down to that awful meal in the basement with the silly chatter of the nurses, and myself on edge all the time to know what was happening upstairs.

'You'll let me know what the doctor says?' I asked Birdie, whom I managed to button-hole on the stairs.

'Why is it such an interest to you?'

'Well, I found him, didn't I?'

'Yes, but that isn't enough for your interest, surely?' Then when she saw that I was in no mood for teasing, 'Oh, all right. I'll do my best, and I'll let you know even if I have to listen at the doors.'

I had to let it go at that.

Much later she brought me the news. The doctor had been and had diagnosed the trouble as brain fag, which might even turn to brain fever if he were not very careful. I knew that he had been over-working for a very long time, and that he had been warned about his health being undermined, but had never had the opportunity to give up. It is very difficult for a big doctor. He has to go on, or to give up for a time and run the risk of being forgotten. I had understood how Ray had felt about this, and how he had gone on and on while there were people who needed his services, with the result that he himself had snapped.

What none of these others realized so acutely was the fact that he had had trouble with his home life, that he had been strung up to breaking-point about Flower, and that he had had to stifle all that and pretend that everything was all right. None of this had helped him.

Quiet was ordered him, perfect rest. He must not be disturbed, whatever happened, and the doctor advised that his wife should be sent for.

I didn't like the sound of that.

'Flower coming back here?' I demanded.

'She is in Vienna,' said Birdie; 'he gave that away before he had time to think. Would you believe it, but Miss Vaughan has already wired for her, and has told her to come back at once. He does not know that, of course.'

'I don't believe that he will want to see her.'

'Oh, of course you know all about it. Tell me something,' besought Birdie.

But I went up to bed.

I could not sleep. I might have guessed all along that he would collapse if he were not careful. A man cannot go on as Ray had been going for so long, working day in, day out, at extreme nervous tension, and all the while with the miserable home to go back to. He had asked me not to leave him when I had first found him only semi-conscious on the stairs, yet the first thing that had happened was that I had been forced to go away.

Sleep was elusive. I tossed and turned, first this way and then that, and all the while I was seeing things out of all proportion, seeing them strangely distorted as they become at night, imagining that he was going to die, and that they would not let me go to him again. Finally towards morning I drifted asleep, to wake with a start when we were called at six.

3

When I went on duty the night nurse told me that Ray had had a fairly good night, and that the doctor had 'phoned through about him and was quite pleased over the report. Meanwhile there had been a cable from Flower which said that she was coming from Vienna by air.

'She must be keen,' said Birdie.

'She must want something,' I thought.

'If you ask me,' said Birdie, waxing confidential, 'there is something more in it than we thought.'

I did not like to tell her that it all seemed to be like coincidence, because on opening the morning paper I had seen the announcement of Bill Dawson's engagement. He was marrying a well-known society heiress who had been left a fabulous fortune by her father the year before, and of course the papers were making a lot of chat about it. They had a whole column of publicity, and it was announced that there had been some hint of the 'romance' in the evening editions of last night.

I thought to myself that Flower must have seen that announcement, and having seen it, she had probably got her white hyacinths and had realized that the game was up. She had quite likely decided to come back from Vienna before she had ever known that her husband was ill, because I could never believe that his illness would disturb her very much.

Only, as I realized too truly, if the affair with Bill were at an end, then she might turn again to Ray. It would be terrible if they tried to pick up the broken pieces of their marriage and make them whole. Somehow I had not thought of such a thing happening until now, and it struck me sharply.

Nothing ever went right in my life. I ought to have gone abroad before any of this happened. I ought to have gone right away, where this sort of thing could not hurt me any more.

I went on duty. Tenny was in charge of Ray, and very full of her job.

'Let me see him!' I begged.

She shook her head.

'I can't, Dallas. The doctor said that he was

to be kept as quiet as possible, and there were to be no visitors. Don't ask me to do it.'

I knew it was unfair to ask her any more, but oh, how I wanted to go inside his room and see with my own eyes how he looked. It was to be an interminable day for me. I had to go about my ordinary routine work, and all the time I was worried to death as to how Ray was getting on. Flowers had to be arranged. Patients had to be washed and made trim for the day. Visitors were ushered in and ushered out again. Mercifully there were no operations; I was glad of that, because I do not believe that I could have concentrated on any serious work.

His patient with the bad appendix asked where he was, and I tried to put her off with a story.

'You're getting better these days,' said I, 'and you can't expect him to be popping in all the time to see you. This is the first step in the right direction.'

I must have sounded very truthful, for she did not doubt me for a moment.

'I'd never have got on so well with any other doctor,' she said.

I agreed.

'I hope he'll come in to-morrow,' she said, a trifle wistfully.

'Oh, I expect he will be along, but you know he does get called away to urgent cases in the country—you can't claim all his time.'

On and on with the work, and all the time I was so desperately anxious for him that I hardly knew what to do. When anyone is ill, then you realize how deeply you care for them.

It was in between answering bells and flying about on duty that I got word about him from Tenny.

'He's doing all right,' she whispered as she passed me; 'he sleeps a lot and he has been asking for you.'

'Tenny, you must let me go to him!'

'I daren't.'

'Tenny, be sporting over this. Risk it, and I'll take the blame for it.'

'Yes, and supposing that old Vaughan caught us?'

'I've got to see him,' I told her.

But Tenny could be a dragon in her own way, and she was not going to be cajoled into this.

'You're behaving like a fool, Dallas,' she said, 'losing your head over a married man like that. It won't do you or him any good. There is nothing to be gained by it, and the sooner you forget him the better. I've learnt my lesson about men, thank goodness. Don't be an idiot. Learn yours.'

And she turned away from me and went back to his room.

I didn't blame her for being angry. I suppose I was behaving like a fool, but I felt so terribly anxious for him that I could not stop myself. It was almost worse that I had had my training, and knew everything that he might be suffering and all the dangers that might accompany his condition. As I went about during that afternoon I tried to put the whole case out of my mind, but although you can exhort other people to do that, you cannot do it so easily for yourself. I kept thinking of all his symptoms. A man who had worked as Ray had done would not be able to face a really bad illness with impunity. He had been calling on his reserve of strength for too long.

If it turned to brain fever, as Tenny seemed to think it might, then he would never get through. He wasn't a happy man, and the will to make others live was not his own will to live. For the past few months I recognized the fact that he had been fighting against desperate odds. Unless something happened to make his home life happier, he would not want to go on living.

I did not care where I came in in all this, but I did care for him. I would have done anything in the world to help him now, only with my hands tied by the routine of this place it looked as if I could do nothing. Things were badly on my nerves.

Tea-time came, and there were the patients' tea-trays in the lift and the usual sorting out of the visitors. The afternoons are generally slack in the home, and the slackness made it worse for me, for it meant that I had more time to think, which was just what I did not want to do.

I sat on in the nurses' little sitting-room, waiting for the patients' bells to tell me that they had done with their tea or were sick of their visitors, and I felt utterly done.

'If this goes on much longer I shall pass out,' I told myself.

I'd got absolutely on edge.

I did not see Tenny until after tea, when I was beginning the work which ends in coming off duty. I saw her then for a moment in the corridor.

'Tenny, how is he?'

'He is doing a great deal better than I should have expected.'

'I must see him.'

'Dallas, don't be so silly. It can't be done; besides, it isn't any of your business. His wife is coming, and she will be here any time now.'

It was all very well of Tenny being so hard about it all, and I caught at her arm. 'You really must help me—one little peep is all I want.'

'Yes, and have Vaughan, or Sister, or someone catch us.'

'I don't care if they do; it is worth it.'

In that moment I realized that she was melting a little. I saw that she was inclined to help me, but frightened in case there were any consequences of doing it.

'I'll see what I can do. The surgeon is there

now, and Miss Vaughan and that Sister Duke. You can't go in for a little while, but I'll let you know if there is a hope,' and she bustled off again with the late tea-tray for number forty-one.

Well, I'd won her round, anyway, and that was one good thing, though it was dreadful waiting to see him. And all the time there was the horrid uncertainty that Miss Vaughan might be going her rounds and getting Tenny scared, so that she was too frightened to let me in at the last minute.

A girl came out of a patient's room across the landing. Her sister was in for an operation the next morning, and they had got very frightened about it. I could see that her face was white and drawn as she came to the lift and pressed the bell. Seeing me, she hesitated.

'Oh, could I speak to you for a moment, Nurse?' she asked.

That was when I remembered the training and the old teaching of my first matron (God bless her), that I was a nurse first. I think that was when I realized that all my feelings for Ray were selfish ones, and that I had a duty to fulfil to my other patients, and to this girl who was so dreadfully anxious about her sister. The routine which went on and which drove me frantic at times, so that I chafed against it and wanted to break free, was something of which I was very definitely part. It was not any use trying to draw back. This routine had got me wholly, and I was a cog in the wheel.

'Is my sister going to be all right? I mean, is it a very dangerous operation?'

She told me all about it; they were everything to one another, and the need for this operation had suddenly parted them, when they had never before been away from one another for a single night of their lives. I tried to comfort her as best I could, and suddenly she turned impulsively and took my hand.

'You're different from the other nurses. They just leave me scared. They seem like machines, but you seem to be human. You must have suffered yourself to know how dreadfully worried I am about this.'

'She is going to be all right. Somehow I feel that, and I am generally right when I get a hunch about the patients. She'll do finely, so don't get too worried about it.'

She was quite gay as the lift took her down the stairs. So she thought I had suffered, and I hadn't. Not until recently. Oh, yes, I'd been lonely and unhappy at times—who isn't?—but I had never felt quite so desperate, quite so hopeless as I had done since I had met Ray Harper. And it wasn't right.

I remembered what I had thought the very first time that I had seen him. Just as though somebody pulled aside a curtain, some unseen showman giving a display of life. Up with the curtain. Lady! this is love!

I pulled myself together with a jerk.

I mustn't be crazy.

4

I saw Tenny standing at the bottom of the stairs, and she was calling to me.

'Dallas.'

I ran to her, because I knew that she had come to tell me I might have a peep at her patient. Miss Vaughan had rustled away into the distance. She was having her anxious moments over a hernia on the second floor, which would possibly keep her busy for a bit. Day Sister had trailed down in her wake, very important, very full of the cases.

'The door is open.' Tenny had caught hold of my arm. 'Take a peep inside and see how he looks. I left it like that for you.'

'You're a dear!'

I went across the landing. On the right was the blanket cupboard built into the wall, and by the side of it his door flung wide open. It was a plain room, as all our rooms were, but this one had no flowers in it. The other patients had them by the thousand, stacks of them—weren't we always carrying them up the stairs and arranging them? But this room had nothing in it to break the prim whiteness of the walls. He was lying on his side and breathing comfortably. I knew at once by the way that he lay that he was not terribly ill. You can tell these things when you are trained. I took note of all the different points about him—his colour, the way his head sank into the pillow, his attitude and breathing. It was a reassuring glance. He was not in a serious condition at all; it was more weakness than anything, sheer collapse.

I was going to cross the threshold when Tenny came up behind me and caught my arm.

'Come away, they're here.'

'Who are here?'

'I thought old Vaughan had gone down to that hernia case, and half-way she must have got the message. It's his wife. She is bringing his wife up to see him.'

At that very moment I could hear the lift rising to our floor and knew that there was no time to make my get-away. Miss Vaughan had realized from the first that I wanted to see Ray, and she would know what I was doing on this floor. Besides, there was Flower. I knew then that I simply could not meet Flower like this.

'I can't!' I gasped, though what that would convey to Tenny I didn't know. Then I acted on a sudden impulse.

Tenny had only time to say 'I told you not to come,' when I opened the door of the blanket cupboard and stepped inside. There was warmth, the strong, steamy warmth of hot pipes, and that queer woolly smell of blankets that are airing. I thought for a moment that the fluff would choke me. Then I realized that I could see through the chink of the door everything that was happening on the landing, and that for the time being I was safe. Miss Vaughan was far too busy to think of coming to the blanket cupboard; besides, it was not the time of day when more blankets were wanted.

I could see Tenny standing on the threshold of the room with the open door, smoothing down her apron and setting her cap pertly to rights. Then the lift doors opened, and Miss Vaughan came out first; she always walked with dignity, as though she were entering a church. All the same, as I saw her coming towards the room I felt that something was wrong. She was not so complacent as usual; she was anxious, and I had the feeling that she did not approve of Flower.

Behind her walked Flower herself.

She looked radiant. I suppose it was because I had never seen her in robust health before that I was so struck with her beauty. She wore a soft green velvet frock and a close-fitting little hat under which her hair curled luxuriously. Flower was delicately made up, exactly like her name; her green velvet coat was collared in chinchilla, diamonds blazed on her fingers. She was a lovely girl, and she had exquisite taste and knew how to emphasize that loveliness of hers. As she passed the cupboard where I was hiding, and by this time quaking in every limb, because it would be too dreadful if Miss Vaughan found me, and so undignified, I smelt the fragrance of the deep purple violets which Flower wore pinned into her collar. It was a destroying beauty, this loveliness of hers, something which demanded and sucked everything up into itself.

They went into the bedroom and the door closed on them. Tenny shut it swiftly and silently, and on that same instant opened the cupboard where I was hiding.

'Quick, Dallas! Oh, I *knew* something would happen. What a fright you gave me!'

I did not answer.

I had seen him for an instant; he had not seen me. Now his wife was in the room with him, his wife and Miss Vaughan, and there was nothing for me to do but to go away and try to forget them.

As it happened, it was that night that I got a letter which surprised me quite a lot. I had had the literature from the Crown Agents, and had written to them again saying that I might consider a post abroad, but had supposed that it would end there. I had had a note from them saying that there was a shortage of trained nurses, but never thought that it would lead to more. Going off duty and downstairs to dinner, I found an important-looking note pigeon-holed in my rack, and opening it saw that it was an offer of a post abroad. There was a job going in

Malta, where they wanted nurses. There was some literature with the mention of this post, and I saw pictures of an island so different and so remote that it rather attracted my attention. A little island at the very foot of Europe, with the palms and the little boats in the harbour, and the hills in the distance, and the offer of escape that came with it.

One could forget there.

Tenny was sitting in the little room afterwards, and I dropped the booklet into her lap.

'What do you think of that?' I asked.

She thought such a lot of it that she could not stop talking about it. Why, it would be too utterly marvellous, said she. Let us write and accept it at once. In Malta it did not rain as it did here in London. Tenny had gone out for a couple of hours that afternoon and had ruined a new hat, so she felt a bit sore on this subject. There would be the Services there, and a gay life. She had always heard of it as being one of the brightest spots where one could really have fun. What a piece of luck, said she.

I was not so sure. I wanted to know more, and it took me three or four days before I got the information that I required.

During those days I made no attempt to see Ray, and I knew that Flower was visiting him. I tried to absorb myself in some really hard work. The girl whose sister had been so anxious on her account went through a bad time. The operation was more involved than we had expected, and when she was opened up there were complications. It was a long and difficult operation, and the man doing it had not got Ray's methods, nor his swiftness. When I handed her over to Birdie for the night I was worried about her, because I felt that there was the chance of her slipping through our hands.

All the next day we fought for her life. Her sister pretended that I had saved her, but I think that it was she herself who did it. They had not much money, those two, and the actual cost of being in the home was a big strain on their slender finances. But they had pluck. They had grit. They had love, too, a splendid and shining love which had brought them through all their troubles.

I can tell you that they taught me a lot in the way that they weathered the storm between them.

Sometimes when you are a hard-up nurse, moving from patient to patient, you get so sick of the extravagance of it all. Women who have nothing to grumble about, yet who make such a fuss. The satin nighties and the masses of flowers. I had grown to hate orchids. Yet these two girls had none of the trimmings of life; they went through a dreadful time of pain and bewilderment and fear and had no flowers. They made do. They had love, though, and it was a love bright enough to last them through their trouble; they had the full appreciation of life; they had one another.

Then I had news of Ray.

'He is recovering marvellously,' said Tenny when I popped into the nurses' sitting-room, where she was having a cup of tea.

'And he's going to get right?'

'Quite all right. You would not have thought that he had such a store of power of resistance on which he could draw, but he had.'

'And Flower?'

Tenny shot me a doubtful look.

'I think it is going to be all right about them. I've thought a lot, and he is so lovely; he is the kind of man who deserves everything, the very best of life. He ought to have had children.'

'I can't see that idea appealing to Flower.'

'Well, frankly, I can't, but I think he has the idea that he can. They've patched up their quarrels and they are like lovers now. You would never think that she had that affair with Bill.'

Tenny went on stirring her tea, and I thought how cruel it all sounded. But there was Malta. However I might hate the idea, it was the wise thing to go away, right away.

'You know, Dallas,' said Tenny, 'I've thought about you and the doctor a lot, and it won't do you any good hanging round him. You may love him, but you have got to think of yourself, too, you know. He is attractive. Heaven knows I realize that. Bill was attractive to, but that didn't help me any.'

I could not see any connection between her affair with Captain Dawson and mine with Ray, but I did not like to say so. Poor Tenny!

I said, 'I'm going to accept that post in Malta, and when they send me the papers I'm signing. What about you?'

'Dallas, there is nothing I'd like better. We could go out there together.'

'And start life all over again. No Bills, no handsome doctors,' and I tried to laugh.

'Do you really mean it? I mean are you pulling my leg, because I don't think I could bear that.'

I shook my head. 'No, I mean it. The papers ought to be here to-night. I shall sign and then give in my notice to Miss Vaughan.'

'I'll do the same.'

She was tremendously excited by the idea, and we both waited for the evening post to come in. When it arrived there was the very letter that I had reckoned on, and the intimation that the posts were still going. I filled my name in quite deliberately. I had to join up before six weeks were through. They gave particulars of where to get special uniform, and of ships that would be sailing. My notice to Miss Vaughan would take a month.

'Her face will be a picture,' said Tenny,

scrawling her name with a flourish; 'she will just fall through her chair with horror. She thinks her home is the place of places, the pearl of homes, and that anybody who has the chance to nurse one of her patients should not look any further.'

'I shall tell her in the morning.'

'I'll ask for an interview just after you. I wish we could persuade Birdie to come too. It would be lovely if *all* the nurses resigned on the same day,' and her gay imagination went wandering off into space.

Tenny was taking no risks, and she insisted that we should post the letter that night. I wanted to demur, but really I had no possible excuse for it. If I were going to burn my boats behind me, the sooner I got on with it the better, so I let Tenny run out to the postbox at the corner, and when she came back realized that now I really had done it.

'That's that,' said Tenny joyously; 'and now for seeing Miss Vaughan in the morning. She is going to have a fit.'

Tenny's amusement over the horror that Miss Vaughan was going to suffer was a very childish affair. She had never got on well with the Matron, and disliked some of her methods and her fondness of routine, so that it amused her enormously to think that such a routine was going to be disturbed.

Miss Vaughan never thought that any nurse

could resign for any reason save ill-health, and would know that both of us were strong and fit, therefore she would be scandalized at the thought that we had given up because we did not care for the home and had found an appointment that we thought we should like better.

When we went to bed soon after nine (we were usually too exhausted to stay up later), Tenny was still chuckling to herself. 'Dream of Malta,' she told me. 'We are going to have the most wonderful time there. I am quite sure that we have taken a step that we shall never regret.'

But I didn't dream of Malta when eventually I got to sleep.

## 5

I asked to see Miss Vaughan immediately after breakfast. As I went down to keep the interview, I saw for a fleeting moment that Flower was in the lift. She was looking radiant in blue with a bunch of white violets pinned at her throat. Directly I saw those flowers I linked them up with memories of her visit to the home as a patient, and I thought, 'I wonder if she is up to her old tricks and going on with that intrigue after all.' Then I dismissed the idea.

I went on into the little sitting-room. There was Miss Vaughan seated in state at her desk, from which she always had her nurses on the mat.

'Well, Nurse?' said she.

If I stayed here a hundred years I should be Nurse, just Nurse always. I couldn't bear it.

I explained that I wanted to tell her in a month's time I should be starting out for an appointment abroad. Tenny had been quite right about this worrying her. She turned pink, and then said that she was grieved to hear that I was dissatisfied with the home, and much more grieved to think that I had gone entirely behind her back and had made arrangements to take on another appointment when a little talk might have put everything right between us. She asked why I had been dissatisfied here. That put me into a very awkward position, and I floundered a good deal, after which she stiffened.

She said, 'Perhaps, Nurse, I notice more than you think, and it has been very unfortunate that matters have turned out the way they have done. If you think a change will be beneficial to you, then it is a change that you ought to make. I have no more to say about it,' but I knew that she was most dreadfully offended.

I said that I was sorry and went off upstairs, to find Tenny just coming down for her appointment.

'What did she look like? How did she take it?' gasped Tenny.

'Not too well.'

'She'll take my resignation worse. I've been

here longer than you have, and she thinks that she has got me on a string, which is just where she is wrong. Now for it,' and she launched herself off towards the little private room.

When she came back again her eyes were twinkling. Tenny was enjoying the chance of a fresh adventure and the hope that now life would jog out of its old routine and give her something to entertain her.

'She looked sick as mud,' said she. 'Now it only needs another to do the same thing, and she will probably swoon. I'm enjoying this.'

I don't believe that Tenny was ever really cut out for a nurse. She enjoys life too much. Looking at her as she stood there, bubbling over with excitement, it seemed hard to remember that anything so sweet should have suffered so badly with Bill. It seemed hard that she had ever had any of the kicks from life when hers ought to be all fun.

I couldn't help feeling sorry for Miss Vaughan. She was a stiff old thing, I know, but it must be a pretty responsible job running a nursing home like that, and to lose two of your nurses in one fell swoop cannot be too amusing.

'You don't tell me that you *like* her?' cried Tenny. 'Oh, dearie me, whatever next?' and she went back to her floor singing.

Well, this was all going to end!

No more up and down the stairs, with anxious people arriving and less anxious people going. You do your best for your patients, and their gratitude is your reward; you nurse them back to health, yet they are always glad when the time to leave you comes, and they can pass out of the doors of the home into the world again. I suppose that is only natural, and I should be glad myself.

That day I heard that Ray would be soon well enough to leave. I had the feeling when Miss Vaughan told me that she knew more than I thought, and that she was sorry for me and wanted to help me, yet could not do so. It was merely an instinctive feeling; there was nothing that she did to bear it out, but all the same I was sure that it was there.

She told me on the stairs.

'As you nursed Mrs. Harper, and have done so much good work for him, I thought that you might like to know,' she said.

'I should like to know very much indeed.'

'I think that I can safely say that all his troubles are ended now; they have made up their differences of opinion. It was a sad thing that his marriage should be so unhappy, but now there is no reason why it should not be quite happy, because the other man is being married at once.'

All the while I knew that her eyes watched mine, and that they were searching eyes, sincere and truthful. She was not saying this with the idea of deliberately hurting me; I knew that.

She was telling me because she believed that it would be kinder and wiser to tell me the truth and to allow that truth to close the door for ever on all chances of romance.

Lady! this is love! And down comes the curtain.

She went on quite clearly: 'I suggested that they should try another honeymoon together and start all over again. They are leaving the home to-morrow, and will be going to the South of France. The doctors want him to have an entire rest away from all work, and there, under happy conditions, they ought to get to know one another better. It ought to signify the fresh start.'

I said, 'Quite so, Miss Vaughan,' and hoped very much that my eyes did not show how deeply I felt all this.

There was a long silence, then she said in a low voice, 'I felt I wanted you to know. You are a very brave girl, Nurse, but you are now running away from something which does not exist.'

I flinched then.

Her sympathy and appreciation was something that was entirely unexpected. Instantly I realized that she had been blind to nothing, and that she had known about us from the very beginning.

She put out a hand.

'I dare say you wonder how it is that I know,

but years ago much the same thing happened to me. I thought then that I should never get over it, and that my heart was broken. It wasn't. Hearts do not break so easily, and I've gone on and I am proud that I have had the strength of mind and of purpose to continue. It was the only thing that I could do, but it wasn't easy to force myself to it at the time.'

I still stood there, dumbly staring at her. I did not know what to say; there seemed to be no solution.

'It is never easy to do the brave thing,' she said, 'but it is the only satisfactory course to pursue. Now I know that the man I loved is a happy and successful surgeon. He was restored to his wife and they have children, which have made all the difference to their lives. I hope very much that this will happen to the Harpers. If they had children then their difficulties would be smoothed away and they would be happy.'

I agreed with her.

She dismissed me then, going on down the stairs, and I went away to my duties in a daze. After all, she was a great woman. Because of her greatness she understood, and it was that understanding of hers which carried her so far. It was to that understanding that I attributed the success of her home, and her management of her nurses and of her patients.

So she knew!

So she also had suffered!

I wanted to go away and cry all by myself, but I knew that this could not be. I had my patients to consider; perhaps that was the best thing of all. I had to go on as she had to, and perhaps the knowledge of responsibility was going to help me bear my burden in the future.

Only it was awful to think that I should be so alone. So desperately alone for always.

CHAPTER FIVE

## AFTERMATH

Tenny and I got out for a couple of hours and went to buy some new uniform, because we should want this for Malta. It is always a joy to get new clothes, even if it is the same old uniform, and for this great occasion I had withdrawn some money out of the post office savings bank for the expedition.

It was a glorious spring day, one of those days when it is good to be alive and when you feel, however drab and dull life has been so far, there is something worth seeking ahead. We went along chattering together, and when we arrived at the shop we had a very happy hour choosing things. I must say uniform has improved enormously since I was trained. Then it was all dull, as dull could be; nowadays it is something that you can choose with a relish. Thank heaven those stiff collars have been abolished, and those starched caps. And those awful strings! When I was first promoted to strings in hospital I thought I could never bear them. They have to be so starched that they cut right into your chin.

'Like Queen Vic,' said Tenny gaily, 'who when she was a child had holly leaves stuck into her bonnet strings to teach her to hold her head up.'

Really, they did do some barbarous things even in her time!

As we came out of the shop with the idea of treating ourselves to tea at a little tea place we knew of where they had the loveliest cream cakes, we ran straight into a very bronzed man who was passing the door. I pulled up with a jerk, but he wasn't looking at me; he was staring at Tenny.

'Why, it's little Jill!' said he.

It seemed so funny to hear Tenny being addressed as little Jill that I almost wanted to laugh. It didn't seem at all right. She had come to a standstill and was looking at him with bewildered eyes. I think that was when I smelt a rat, and saw something which at that particular moment was probably not seen by either of them. The man looked as if he had returned from some distant country; he was brown with a brownness that men do not get here even in the summer.

'It's Hugh!' she said.

'Yes, it's Hugh all right. What are you doing here? Not still nursing? Oh, my dear, why ever did you stick to it? What a waste of a gay youth!' Then he glanced at me. 'A friend?' he asked. 'Look here, we can't talk in the street. Come along and have some tea.'

Before we could say no he had called up a taxi and we were going off to the May Fair. He was, it seemed, an old love of Tenny's; they had lived near one another when she was a little girl in sandals, and he a young sub. in the army. He had gone to India, and he was home now on furlough. He was a colonel. 'But pray heaven I don't look like it,' he said.

Sitting comfortably in the May Fair, we told him about our Maltese project. We were very sick of the home, sick of a life spent in carting about trays and doing dressings, and always the eternal flow of patients, and never getting out for very long, and we had decided to throw our bonnets over the windmill.

'And very wise too,' said he; but all the while I could see that he had no eyes for anybody but Tenny.

I realized that I was playing gooseberry, which is not a very nice feeling. I was the third in the party, and I am sure that they would much rather not have had me there at all, but I could think of no excuse that I could concoct whereby I might slip away. I could think of nothing which would give me the chance to escape.

Tenny was dimpling and blushing. She looked very pretty. I have often envied Tenny her looks. Of course, I'm one of those people who never look anything, but she has soft red-brown hair and grey eyes, with a brown fleck in them. Tenny has a dimple, too, a sweet and lovely dimple which pops up whenever she is amused.

It was very restful sitting there in the hotel and knowing no bell could jar in on us, and no lift could arrive demanding immediate attention for some patient. I quite forgot that time was on the wing and that we were both due back on duty.

I sprang up.

'Good heavens, Tenny, look at that clock.'

'We shall both be on the mat.'

He said, 'Look here, it can't end here. We have got to meet again. What about a dinner—what about a theatre?' and then, glancing nervously at me, 'Both of you?'

'I'm on night duty,' I lied valiantly.

I knew that Tenny wanted to giggle, but she buttoned her mouth down primly and said, 'Well, one evening I could get out.'

'To-morrow?'

'All right. To-morrow. Is there any show you particularly want to see?'

'I've seen nothing,' he said.

She was in a hurry to get away because Nurse Tops was looking out for us, and she was one of those martyrish people who make such a frightful fuss if you are five minutes late. We both knew what we should get when we got home, so that we were impatient to start.

'Shall I choose?' he asked.

'Anything will be nice.'

'Can you manage dinner to-morrow night at seven-thirty?'

'I don't get off duty until then.'

He said, 'Then we'll cancel the show and go and dine at the Casino. Eight-thirty there? I'll meet you in the foyer.'

That was when we broke away.

We almost ran back, and there was not time for Tenny to explain anything. It is a very criss-cross journey to our part of London, and difficult to get to from anywhere, I always think, but we managed to get there only five minutes late, and as we went up to our rooms I panted, 'Who was he?'

Tenny was so out of breath that she could only gasp, 'Old love,' and then started laughing at herself, with the result that she had to sit down before she could make the last five stairs.

And hadn't Nurse Tops got something to say!

As I went my round of the patients, finishing up it suddenly dawned on me that we might not need our uniform for Malta after all. Supposing that Tenny changed her mind and went off with this man? Supposing she went back to India when the furlough was ended? Tenny as a colonel's lady. Imagine it!

I was not sure that I would like tackling Malta all alone. It seems a long way off for a woman who has never been abroad before. It seems almost too far. I did not think that the brightness dazzled me quite so much, and yet I could not stay here. I did not want to stay here and go on with a life which had become so difficult. If Miss Vaughan had guessed that I cared for Ray, then it was probable that everybody else had.

They said nothing because they were too nice, but that did not prevent them thinking things.

No, I had got to get away.

I had got to get right away and forget.

## 2

The next day the Harpers went off together.

Tenny told me that he was going that afternoon, and I was torn two ways—between the dreadful desire to see him go and the knowledge that it would be an infinite torture.

Then in the end I met them on the stairs, and it had been nothing that I had planned. All their arrangements had been altered last thing of all, it seemed, and they were catching an earlier train.

I was returning upstairs from my dinner, and as I got half-way I saw them coming down. Flower came first, a good way ahead of him. Flower in a perky little frock, sprigged gaily with blossoms, and a mink coat flung over her shoulders with that indolence with which only a woman like Flower wears mink.

'Oh, *you*!' she said, and came to a stop.

She took me entirely by surprise.

She took me so much by surprise that I had not the strength of mind to pass her by, nor to realize that I had to face this thing out. I felt my two hot hands go with spread palms against the wall for support. I was grateful for the coolness of it. I was desperately grateful to feel their firmness.

'I hope you are better,' I said at last, and my voice was far away and trembled, quite unlike my own voice.

'You don't hope that at all,' she said. 'You know perfectly well that you wish I had died. Well, I haven't died. I've lived and now we are starting off for our second honeymoon. What do you think of that, Nurse?' and her voice defied me.

It was so like Flower!

I wanted to turn and run from her. I didn't think I could bear more, but there is a certain desperate pride which stands firm in a person, and that held me.

I said, 'I am very glad, and I hope that you

both will be very happy.'

'That isn't true,' she flashed. 'You don't hope anything of the sort, and you know it!'

'Please, Mrs. Harper, do try to think of me more charitably. I did my best for you.'

'Because you thought you would get round my husband that way.'

'It was nothing of the sort. It was my duty to my patient put under my charge. I hope that I have never yet failed in my duty.'

Perhaps my quietness surprised her, for she stared at me for a moment as though she could not understand me, and then saying, 'Oh, you make me tired,' passed on.

She flounced down the stairs, leaving a trail of gardenia essence behind her. Slowly I went upstairs and that was how I met him face to face.

I had been so disturbed by the stormy meeting with her that I had not thought of this. Even when I had met Flower I had never thought that I should meet him too, because patients always leave us by the lift. I cannot imagine what induced him to come down the stairs, unless it was that perhaps he thought he might see me. But then I may be flattering myself.

He was standing on the top stair, thinner, paler, a little nervous about his feet.

'Oh, doctor!' I exclaimed; and then, 'Won't you take my arm? You ought not to be coming down these stairs alone; they'll be too much for you. Why didn't you go down in the lift?'

He smiled, his old, kind smile.

'Thank you very much. I got sick of my room, and was trying to follow Flower down. I'm a bad patient, I dare say, but I wanted to see the stairs again, and I hate your lift. They always say that doctors are the worst patients, don't they?'

There was a certain joy about feeling him as he leant on me. A certain satisfaction to know that my strength could be of use to him, my own full, abundant health help him now. He leaned hard. He leaned, and I could feel his muscles straining. He must have been considerably weakened by his illness, and have suffered more than I had ever supposed.

He said in a low voice:

'We are going to make a new start. Miss Vaughan is a very wonderful woman in some ways, a very understanding woman.'

'She is great,' I said. 'She sees more than anybody ever imagines. Now take it gently; there is no need to hurry.'

Down we went very slowly.

'Perhaps I was a little intolerant of Flower, perhaps I was unkind,' he said; 'anyway, I am trying to make up for all that now. Lying up there I have had lots of time for thinking, and perhaps I have seen some of my mistakes. I feel rather a cad.'

We came to the last bend in the stairs. For a moment his hand rested on mine.

'Dallas, you do forgive me?' he said weakly.

'I have nothing to forgive,' I answered.

He was ill. I knew now that he was nothing like as convalescent as the others thought, and that he had no right to be leaving the home at all. Standing in the hall were Flower and Miss Vaughan. Turning, they saw us coming.

Flower gave a little scream.

'I might have known as much,' she said.

It was Miss Vaughan who, ignoring that, came forward and took Ray's other arm.

'He was coming down alone, and was not fit,' I explained, and she accepted this explanation.

'You were quite right,' she said, and she meant it as a dismissal back to my floor.

I turned and went.

I wanted to look back. Heavens, how I wanted to look back, and yet had to steel myself against it. No, the thing had got to end here. He had his wife, I had my career. He would come back well, and I should go to Malta. We should probably never meet again, which was the best way out.

When he returned, firmly established with his wife, he would be back to the operating theatre, back to haunt the stairs, bringing me into constant and daily contact with him. It had been far better to go. Miss Vaughan had said that I was brave, but this was not courage. I was running away because I was afraid.

'So that's the end,' said Tenny. 'Never mind, you'll be gone by the time that he returns. You'll have forgotten a lot, too. It seems hard now, but time is an enormous healer.'

It was easy for her, she had her colonel, who would be taking her out to the Casino that night. She had more than I had.

I didn't try to vindicate myself.

3

In a month we should start for Valletta.

In one month I should be turning my back on England, and setting off for a new land, where there would be bluer seas and brighter skies and a new race of people.

Meanwhile Tenny spent every spare moment with Hugh. He would be returning to India a fortnight after we sailed for Malta, if we ever were to sail; I had an idea that this might get held up. It was quite obvious to me from the first that Hugh was terribly attracted to Tenny, and although she refused to think of anything like that, I realized that she had a St. Martin's summer that she could dispose of. Her first love had been Bill, and hard though it might seem, it always would be Bill. I believe that there is something about a first love which does not come again—a brightness, a quality which is too precious. But what she could give to Hugh was possibly a more enduring emotion. It was something sweeter still.

'Oh, that's just nonsense,' she said.

But of course it wasn't nonsense! She told me a fortnight later, when our passages were booked and when everything was actually in readiness. I was arranging some Riviera flowers in the nurses' sitting-room, and all the time I was wondering how the other two were getting on on the Riviera, when Tenny burst in.

She said, 'I've got to tell you, Dallas—it's Hugh.'

'I've known all along,' I admitted, and it was the truth.

'Why, I never knew. I couldn't believe it. He has been so frightfully unhappy and so lonely. It's going to be rather wonderful, Dallas, only it worries me about Malta. You'll throw up the whole thing now, and it will be my fault. You oughtn't to stay on here; it is all wrong for you, with Dr. Harper coming back and working here. Yet I feel you won't go away without me.'

I said I'd try.

After all, I knew as well as she did that I couldn't stay on in the home, and that she was quite right. It would be impossible to go on meeting him.

'I'll go,' I said.

She didn't know the tremendous resolution that demanded of me. It was something almost too big for me, because I realized how lonely that journey would be.

'You will? Oh, Dallas, then I can marry Hugh happily. I can feel quite gay about it. It was the idea that I was letting you down. It was the thought that it would spoil all your plans.'

'I'll be all right. After all, I'm grown up, and we have to make our own way in life. I can't always expect to have a companion with me.'

She flung her arms round me and kissed me. 'Oh, Dallas, you're a brick! I'm going to be so happy, and I do hope you'll meet somebody like Hugh in Malta.'

I didn't hope that. I'm very much the one-man girl, I'm sure, and I didn't see myself meeting anybody else.

'It won't be like that,' I said.

'You never know. It might be. There was a time when Bill absolutely absorbed me and I could have sworn that there would never be anybody else. But I got over that. Now I can't think how I ever came to think of Bill at all. You'll feel like that about Ray. You will, really.'

But it never seemed to me that you could compare the two men, for Bill had always been quite a different type.

She and Hugh asked me out to sup with them, and I went one night because I could not go on refusing. It was all very different from the life that I was used to, very restful and calm. I envied Tenny. She had had her bad time but now she was going to have her good time. They were very much in love though I don't suppose that she realized it, because Tenny still believed that she had given her best to Bill. What she had given him was just infatuation, a mad moment or two, and then a loyal clinging to a memory. It was never anything more.

I should be setting out for Malta, and alone. It needed some pluck to face that journey and to start a fresh life under different conditions, conditions which as yet I did not understand in the least. But Miss Vaughan had said that I had courage. It was the courage that I was drawing on now.

## 4

Then one day I saw that I was down for duty in the theatre. I saw the little notice in the report book when I came on duty, my name as the nurse, the patient's name, the disease and then the surgeon.

It was Ray!

'I can't,' I told myself quickly, 'I can't face that.'

I had gone through the agony of seeing him go into the hall to his wife, and, as I had thought out of my life for ever, now it looked very much as though I had got to see him again. They must have come back from the Riviera sooner than they had been expected. In that moment I thought of pretending to be ill. I have never malingered before and it was of course a dreadful thing to think of now. Then I remembered that we were already short of nurses in the home, for it was holiday time and a Sister and another nurse had gone away. There would be nobody to take my place.

I had to get my patient ready, and she was in a panic, little knowing the horror that was in me.

Perhaps her alarm made me feel better, or at least decided me to take a grip of myself.

'It makes it easier to know that you are going to be with me,' she said, 'you will hold my hand, won't you?'

How could I fail her?

A nurse has a duty to her patient, and that comes before self. I knew that then.

When she had her first dose of nerve soother which they always give them first, I laid her hand in mine and felt the pressure of her fingers in a grateful response. I went on holding fast to it long after she herself was entirely unconscious. I helped the anæsthetist to carry her, holding her head, and I laid her on the table. She looked like a child.

Then I saw Ray for the first time since he had left to start life again. He was standing there waiting for the anæsthetic to take effect. Ray, in his white overall with his hands grotesquely dark in their rubber gloves. Ray, who might have been any man in the world, and yet I knew all the time that he was my man. *I knew that.*

He could not cheat me, because although there was the linen mask across his mouth, I could see his eyes.

They were still hungry.

They were not the eyes of a man who had found satisfaction or happiness, or any of the things that he had been seeking on a second honeymoon. They were the eyes of a man in Hell.

I knew instantly that the whole affair had not been a success, and that Flower had probably failed him again. She did not understand loyalty. She did not understand truth. He was standing on the threshold of a difficult future and I had to brave myself to withstand that pleading in his eyes. The affair had not ended as I thought, even though I did leave for Malta.

All through the operation my heart was not in my work. I was standing there thinking, 'What is the good of our going on like this? What is the use of pretending about it like we both are doing? Why should I go away to a new country and be lonely, and lose my friends and everyone else just so that Flower should go on making us both so desperately unhappy?' Surely the happiness of two people is far more important than that of one?

Happiness.

It seemed as though this were the golden butterfly which it was impossible for any of us to capture.

I knew now as I stood here, outwardly so calm beside the operating table, that from this point onwards we had reached the pitch of snapping. I was getting out; I was quitting, and the thing I wanted most in this world was to stay and fight the whole affair out to its bitter end.

I knew that I could not bear to have stayed on seeing Ray day after day, intimately and closely going about our mutual work in the home. It was asking too much of any woman. I had stood it so long, but I just could not stand it any more.

The operation finished.

The last stitch was in place; the bandages were folded round the limp body by Ray, always insisting on doing everything himself. He was most meticulous in the bandaging of his patients, and I had watched those deft fingers working too many times before.

She was on the stretcher now, and being lifted gently away. There was the sound of a starched frock rustling after her; the clink as the anæsthetist gathered up his things; Sister making her adieu. I was left. I was tidying up the theatre, because the actual theatre nurse had failed them yesterday; she had gone down with migraine and could not attend to her duties. I was putting things back into place, picking up used swabs and dirty instruments, throwing rubber gloves into the sterilizing jar. One by one the others drifted out, but I knew that he was still left. I thought frantically, 'Surely not here, here of all places?'

Then I knew that it was going to be here! We were alone together for the first time for many a long day.

He had torn off the mask and the cap; he had crumpled up his overall and had flung it aside. He was washing his hands, as I pushed the instruments back into their place on the trolley, then he came towards me drying his fingers on the towel.

He said, 'I did not know that you would be on duty here this afternoon.'

'I did not know that you were back.'

I thought that he was evasive in his reply to that.

'Yes, I'm back. I wish I had never gone away from work, it is all so difficult, all so utterly hopeless.'

'But you are feeling better? You will now keep quite fit, I hope.'

It seemed so silly, so hopeless, this stupid, banal conversation, playing at talking, playing at being natural when both of us were so desperately unnatural.

'You know,' he told me, 'that I am feeling quite dreadful.'

'I'm sorry.'

'We can't go on like this.'

Everything had suddenly come to a climax,

and here we were two people very much in love standing together in the empty theatre still smelling of the anæsthetic, with the last traces of the operation in the bins and in the stained instruments. A man and a woman who had appeared to be machines, but who had been anything but machines at heart.

I said, 'I know we can't go on like this, that is why I have decided to go away. I am leaving here at the end of the week and going to Malta.'

'Away?'

'I must. You say that you can't go on like this, I know that I can't. It isn't fair to ask that much of me. It is so dreadful! I couldn't go on seeing you and knowing how things were. It is far, far better that I should do the wise thing—make a clean break and go.'

He stood there staring at me quite helplessly. Automatically he went on wiping his hands on the towel marked 'theatre towel,' but it was only automatic. I realized that he had not expected this, and that it had been a desperate blow to him. When at last he spoke, he was resigned. He had controlled himself and had got that mask over his face once more; the mask significant of the doctor who does not betray his emotions.

'No, you're right. You are brave about it, far, far braver than I am. Oh, my dear, what a fool I've been all along, but it isn't any use. I'm no good to you, or to myself. There is nothing I can do to put right some of the things that have happened, nothing at all. There isn't any way out, and the part that hurts most is the fact that we have only the one life to live.'

He pushed the towel back into place and rolled down his sleeves.

He said, 'I'm telling the truth now, and I suppose that we shall never see one another again. If you go to Malta it is a long way off, and I have to stay here; this is my bread and butter. But I know that my heart will always be in Malta with you.'

I said nothing. If I had tried to speak I think that I should have broken down, and somehow I did not want this to happen. Tears might be a relief, but they would hurt us both, and goodness knows we had been hurt enough.

He went on.

'The first time I ever saw you I knew that this would happen. I'd been unhappy for so long. Lonely for so long. I've got to go on being unhappy and lonely, there isn't any way out. I'm being full of self-pity, but I can't help feeling sorry for myself, and for you too, Dallas, so much might have been possible, so much might have come to both of us, only that it was too late. Nothing can undo what has happened.'

There wasn't anything that I could say. The thing was ending. It was better that it should end, but I wished we could have spared one another this last scene.

He turned sharply in the doorway and took a last look at me as I stood there, and I think I shall always remember him as he glanced back. Then he walked straight out of the theatre and left me.

I knew that there wasn't anything more for either of us.

Quite mechanically I went on picking up the instruments and putting them on one side ready to be sterilized. Quite automatically the routine of which I had become so much a part went on, but it seemed as though something inside me had stopped dead—something that would never go again.

## 5

I told Tenny that night.

She came into my room for a chat. She had got patterns of frocks, and she was absorbed in her trousseau. Hugh was behaving like a dear, and he knew that she had not got very much put by, so he had paid for this for her.

'I feel like a kept woman,' she said, and laughed. 'He has been so unutterably sweet over everything, but do you think I ought to let him pay?'

'Of course. What does it matter who pays as long as you both are happy?'

She said, 'He has given me so much that I have felt desperately worried about marrying him. You see, Bill has been on my conscience a lot. I've lain awake at night wondering what I ought to say about that, wondering what I ought to do about it.'

I only hoped that she was not going to rake up the earth which buried the corpse of the past. No good could come of that.

'You see,' I said, 'the shutters are closed fast on all that, and nobody wants to remember it. Take my advice and forget it.'

'I couldn't. Some people are made that way; they can draw down the shutters and forget everything that ever happened. I can't. A horrid ghost comes plucking at my sleeve. I kept thinking all the time, "If Hugh knew about Bill he wouldn't marry me." Then yesterday I knew that I couldn't go on with it. I mean on with it without Hugh knowing. I'd got to tell him. That took some courage, Dallas.'

Misguided courage, I felt. She had suffered enough already without giving herself an additional burden to bear. But apparently she could not have rested until she had told him.

'Yes, it wasn't so awful once I had started, but it was rather dreadful getting started. I think he knew what was coming, because after a little while he said there wasn't any need to tell him any more. He had always guessed that there had been somebody, and anyway that somebody had gone right out of my life now, and did not matter any more. He'd like to leave it at that. Oh, Dallas, you may think that I did wrong to tell him, but the enormous relief was something unspeakable! Afterwards when I felt the load lifted, it was just as though I had suddenly got well after a dreadful illness.'

I knew by her face that she was a different Tenny. Always before there had been the feeling that Bill still mattered to her. He didn't matter any longer. I had a firm idea that he would never matter again.

I suppose in her joy she had been blind to the fact that I had something to tell her, then she caught sight of my face and stopped talking about herself.

'Oh, Dallas, I'm being rather a pig. I'd forgotten about you. I've let you down shockingly about Malta, and now I'm letting you down by not listening to what you've got to say. It's about Ray, I suppose?'

'I was theatre nurse when he was operating to-day.'

'And he talked to you?'

'And he talked to me. The second honeymoon was a failure. It must have been dreadful, or he would not have admitted it as he did, as though there was nothing left to live for any more, as though he felt he could hardly go on.'

'Did you tell him about Malta?'

'Yes, I told him about Malta, and he was upset, but he knew it was the best thing for us to do. We could not go on meeting, more especially now that the curtain is up between us, and each realizes how the other one feels. Oh, Tenny, it is so dreadful that we can't do anything to help ourselves.'

'If only Providence would see fit to remove Flower! If only something could have gone wrong in that op. of hers!'

'Don't say things like that!'

'But I'm feeling things like that. She has behaved vilely. If only she had run off with Bill it would have been easier for everybody. And he would have bought a packet full of trouble, too.' She laughed at that. 'It really would serve Bill right after he has played about with anything and everything in a petticoat if he bought it in the end by marrying a Tartar.'

'Perhaps he has married a Tartar, only we don't know it!'

'Perhaps he has.'

It wasn't getting me anywhere. We sat there and we talked, but it was merely going round and round in circles.

In the end I tried to put her mind at ease. 'Tenny, don't think that you have let me down by backing out of Malta. You haven't done. I know it will be lonely and awful for a bit, and I may find the climate difficult and everything will take some getting used to, but I won't let that worry me. The bigger change that I can get the better. It is the only thing to shake me up and make me realize that there is something in life to go on for. I sound melodramatic, but I don't mean it that way.'

'You're being terribly brave.'

'No, I'm not. I feel all squirmy inside, but I'm going on.'

She kissed me before she went. 'I've got a hunch, Dallas, that life has got something nice tucked up its sleeve for you; I have a hunch that it isn't going to end here and that there is a good time ahead. Oh, I do hope it comes true.'

'I hope so, too.'

But I realized then that there was the present moment to be lived through and that the present moment had it in its power to hurt me more than anything else in life. I determined I would not look too far ahead, and I would try to choke down that feeling of squirminess and go forward courageously. To-morrow never comes, they say. To-morrow was coming a great deal too often for me.

I was getting pretty desperate about it all. I wished at that particular moment that I could have a pleasant little nervous breakdown—something that would pop me to bed for a week or two while everything sorted itself out, something which came right in the end.

Only life isn't made as easily as that.

# 6

Suddenly we got a tetanus in the home.

The man came in and developed it almost at once; there we were with the whole home in a flap about it, and everybody naturally thrilled to the core.

'Of course he'll never live,' said Nurse Johnson with great superiority.

'I never thought I'd have the luck to see one of those,' said Birdie.

Extra nurses went off the floors to see to this special case, which meant that others were left with their hands full, with the result that I got precious little time to think about myself, which was probably a very good thing.

It was just what I was wanting—life to pass by in a whirl until I got to Malta. I wanted to forget that there was such a person as myself, or such a man as Ray Harper, and the best way to sink all personal feelings was in work. I had got to work really hard.

The tetanus case in the home made us so busy that it did not look as though I should have much time to think, and when I went off duty for my lunch at twelve Tenny leant over the banister and called after me:

'There has been a telephone message up from downstairs. There is a lady there who has called to see you.'

'To see *me*?'

'So they said.'

'There must be a mistake.'

Sometimes, of course, old patients come back to see us, but more often they forget. A home is useful when one is ill, but the interest soon flags when they get well again, and to come back to visit us is a bother, and reminds them too much of a time when they were in pain.

'George said that he was sending her up to the nurses' sitting-room,' said Tenny, and then she picked up the tray which had just arrived for the patient, and off she popped with it.

I was rather annoyed that somebody should call on me at the first chance I had had for a moment to myself in a very busy morning, and I went along in an ill humour.

Who would it be? I did not care very much. There certainly was nobody whom I wanted to see, because I have very few friends. My life is so very much at the mercy of my patients that I have no time to cultivate friends of my own.

I opened the door swiftly, and shut it again behind me, just as quickly. I heard myself give a quick exclamation, a sudden intake of breath, and then steeled myself to face what I knew was going to be an ordeal.

Flower was standing there.

Her colour was coming and going, and I knew by the darkness of her eyes that she was in a furious temper. She stood before me, steadying herself against the closed door, her arm stretched along it, her eyes surveying me, her lip curling.

'Yes,' she said, 'I wanted to have a word with you.'

I could not think of any reply to make, but stood there, gaping helplessly, as though I were a guilty person.

Then I said, 'I was just going off duty.'

'I dare say, but you won't get round me that way. I have got to see you, whatever you may think about it. It is quite time you and I had a talk.'

I felt my mouth going dry. Flower's face was dreadful, and the crazy look in her eyes quite frightened me.

'I don't know what it is that you want to talk to me about,' I protested.

'You do know. Of course you know. You have been trying to steal my husband from me for some time. You fell in in love with him when you first met him.'

'I have done nothing of the sort.'

'Oh, yes, you have, only you have been so sly over it that most people would not realize it for what it was. You know that you have been aiming at it ever since you met him. What was the good of our going away on a second honeymoon like that, when you intended coming too?'

I thought that she must have taken leave of her senses.

'I come too?' I demanded. 'Such a thing was

never suggested by anybody nor thought of for a moment. I have been here for nearly a year save for the two days that I spent with you down at Ventnor. You know perfectly well that I have never left the place.'

'I know perfectly well that in spirit you came with us. He was always talking about you, always thinking about you, always comparing the two of us. Oh, yes, you played your cards well enough.'

'I've never played any cards.'

'Yes, you have. All women fall in love with him on sight, and he is mine. I've got him. You needn't think that I am going to let him go, because I am not. It's been a nice life for me with a whole body of hysterical women imagining themselves in love with him, with a whole crowd of people going googly-eyed whenever they saw him coming. Oh, the life of a doctor's wife isn't all fun, as you may find out one of these days when you've baited your hook cleverly enough and have landed one of them. But you won't get my man; I intend fighting for him till my last breath. Nothing will ever induce me to let another women have him, even if I don't want him myself.'

She looked at me defiantly.

It was a dreadful moment, because I knew quite well that she was perfectly right in what she was saying. She meant to hold on to Ray tooth and claw, even if it were at the sacrifice of all our happiness. She would hold fast to him, whatever happened, and she would never let him go.

I don't think she cared what anybody suffered as long as she was all right. I don't think she minded even if her own emotions were torn as long as she had the satisfaction of the realization that she was keeping what was her own. She was vindictive. She was one of those lovely women whose beautiful eyes are hard and cold as stones, and they looked right down into me.

I knew that I did not flicker.

I told her then what I felt about her.

'I know what you are, and I know also that even though you may keep him chained to you, it is with a chain of iron, and you will never hold his heart that way. You have played with fire; you have thrown away all the best that he had to give you. You never really cared for him, and now you will never regain his love. You say that he is yours, but his heart is his own, and you'll never have that again.'

'How dare you talk to me like that?'

'I have done nothing of which I could be ashamed,' I said. 'I have the right to say what I think.'

'You have deliberately tried to coax away another woman's husband.'

'I have never tried to steal him.'

'Except when you say that I shall never have

his heart, you are boasting about the success of your cunning,' and her lips curled. 'You may look upon my hold upon him as being a chain of iron, and talk horridly about it, but anyway the law supports that chain of iron, and it looks upon any claim you may think that you have as being a rotten one. You will never have him, not if you go on trying from now until Doomsday.'

'Then there is nothing more to be said.'

I knew that she hated my coldness.

I knew that here was something with which she could not compete, because Flower had never been the type of woman who could fight reserve, and it frightened her. She had hoped to sweep everything before her with bombast, and with her arrogance, and she had not succeeded.

I had been ready for her.

As we stood there I heard the door behind her opening slowly, and saw Miss Vaughan herself standing there framed in the lintels. For one moment I would have put out an involuntary hand to stop Flower going on talking, because she had not heard Miss Vaughan, but she was so furious that she was past seeing what I was doing.

She went on remorselessly.

'I made a mistake in ever coming to this beastly home. I might have known that it was rotten, rotten to the core. You nurses always fall in love with the doctors whom you work for. You are a designing set of hussies, and all the while you try to pretend that you are so good and sweet and so prim, but all the while you know quite well what you are getting at. It is disgusting.'

Miss Vaughan stepped forward.

Her face was more agitated than I had ever seen it before, and she put out a hand and touched Flower on the arm.

'That will do,' she said.

Flower turned sharply and gazed at her in surprise. Then she was so angry that I think it was impossible for her to stop herself. Seeing her in this violent temper of hers, it was easy to imagine what a ghastly life Ray must have had with her, what a terrible lot he must have endured.

She said, 'So you have been spying on me? Listening at the door? Coming sneaking in behind my back? Oh, yes, I thought it was this kind of place from the very beginning. I thought that you were out to get everything that you could out of people by fair means or foul. You were actually stooping to spying, although you don't like my calling it so, but that was what it was.'

'Mrs. Harper, you are overwrought; it isn't wise to disturb yourself so much.'

'I'm not overwrought. For once I have had my eyes opened to a lot of things. This nurse has been trying to take my husband from me.

Oh, you'll defend her, you'll back her up, but it is true. There is a sort of frightful trades union between all you medical people, but all the same you can't diddle with truth. She has come between me and Ray, and what's more I'm going to tell the world about it.'

She gave a last look at us, and then grabbed at her bag and gloves, snatching them up from the table. One of the gloves, a long soft piece of velvet, dropped to the ground, and with courtesy Miss Vaughan stooped and lifted it, handing it back to her.

She accepted it without a word.

I don't know why, but that gentle little act stood out etched in my mind as something that I should not forget in a hurry. The older woman in her prim uniform, with her sadly wise face, offering the glove to the other girl, who flung herself out in a fury.

'Well, now you know what I think of you, both of you,' snapped Flower defiantly.

She opened the door, and I saw her standing there for a moment before she banged out. She slammed it after her, and we could hear her running off down the stairs like a crazy thing. She was quite uncontrolled. I think that we just stood and stared helplessly at one another.

## 7

I felt deeply humiliated, not only for myself, but also for Miss Vaughan, who was so good and sweet and who had never deserved this horrible scene which had been forced upon her.

We stood there staring mutely at one another, then she spoke. She did not reproach me; I think that it might have been almost better if she had done.

'Sit down, my dear. You are over-strung,' she said, and gently pressed me into a chair.

'I'm all right,' I tried to explain.

'Better sit down.'

I believe that her kindness hurt more than anything else. I felt the tears coming, and though for a moment I tried to blink them back, it did not work, and I burst into tears. It was the relief of that tension and the knowledge that Flower had gone. I hoped that I might never see her again. It was something that I did not think that I could bear.

I suppose Miss Vaughan thought that it would relieve my feelings to cry, for she made no attempt to stop me, but let me go on.

Then she said, 'Now you must listen to me.'

'I am very sorry to think that this happened. It wasn't my fault.'

'I know that. I know quite well that she was beside herself, and that she did not know what she was saying.'

'It was terrible.'

'I am glad that you are going to Malta, though when I first heard of the project it worried me. But it seems to me now that it is far better for you to get right away, somewhere where she cannot follow you. She is a dreadful woman. A temper like that borders on madness.'

I heard myself murmuring tearful gratitude. Then, when I could control myself a little better, I felt that I had to tell her something about it, even if she did not want to hear.

'Do believe me, Miss Vaughan, when I tell you that none of this had been my fault. There has been nothing wrong in what has happened, nothing that either of us could help or avoid. We have hardly seen one another, and all through it we have been thinking of her.'

'I do believe you.'

'I've got to go away.' I don't think that I even realized that Miss Vaughan was listening, because my thoughts were now running away with me. 'I've got to go right away and try to forget that this happened.'

She held out her hand and took mine.

'My child, I am terribly sorry for you. Words will not help you. Sometimes I think that sympathy is almost harder to bear than reproach. I know you have not been to blame, because I once suffered in like circumstances. You could not have gone on like this, and it is far, far better that you are leaving almost at once and starting in a different place and with entirely different people. Even though it may seem the hard thing to do now, do realize that it will be the right thing in the long run.'

Of course at that particular moment I felt that to go away was like sentence of death. It was banishment. I could not imagine how I should go on with life if I should never see Ray again, nor hear his voice, nor talk to him.

'Believe me,' she said, 'the clean break is the only way. It leaves no jagged ends.'

I knew she was right, yet the clean break was going to hurt me far more than anything else. The telephone bell went, and I think that I was glad of something concrete, something which would give me a job to do, so that I might forget myself for a moment. I became a nurse again, a nurse who was still on duty.

'Yes?' I said.

'Is Miss Vaughan up there?'

'Yes, she is with me now.'

'She is wanted down here very urgently. An accident case has been brought in. Will you ask her to come as quickly as possible?'

'Of course.'

I rang off and told Miss Vaughan that she was wanted, and on the instant she stiffened. All that gentle understanding manner seemed to go in the one supreme knowledge that her services were needed. She went off and I heard her footsteps dying away on the stairs.

But in that interview I had seen her heart, and I knew that she was a grand woman, and probably the memory of her greatness was going to help me start the new job better than anything else.

I hoped so.

## 8

I sat on in the nurses' sitting-room, not feeling that I could go down to lunch yet and join the other nurses in the basement dining-room and listen to the fatuous conversation with very visible signs still on my face that I had been crying.

When a bell tinkled I went to see the patient, even though it was not my duty time, but it helped me to prop up her pillows (she had sunk too low in the bed), and she was a friendly, kindly sort of patient, whom I liked.

Then Tenny came in.

'Miss Vaughan sent me up to relieve you,' she said. 'She thought you might be feeling a bit worried about things.'

'To relieve me? But I'm not on duty. I was just going downstairs to get my lunch.'

'Miss Vaughan wants you to go down to her sitting-room.'

That seemed queer to me, and I said so. 'But we have been talking and have said all that there is to say. I don't see why she wants me to go down there? Whatever else is there?'

'She just said that she wanted you to go down to her room at once,' and it struck me as she said it that Tenny was looking a little odd. Her voice did not appear to be natural, and I realized that she was avoiding my eyes.

'Don't be silly,' I said. 'I'm going down to get my lunch.'

'Dallas, please go to Miss Vaughan. Honestly she wants you there, and it is urgent. Something has happened. Do listen to what I am saying—you *must* go down.'

I took another look at Tenny's face and saw that she had gone extraordinarily pale. I don't know why, but with the silly, abrupt reasoning of the brain I suddenly wondered if Ray wanted me. If something had happened to him and now he wanted me to be with him. I turned quickly, and I think I ran all the way down the stairs, though when I got to Miss Vaughan's room I found her standing there quite alone.

Her dignity seemed to have gone. When she had left me to go down to the accident case she had been calm and very professional. Now she was harassed. I knew it the second that my eyes lit on her; she was agitated about something that had happened.

'Sit down, please,' she said.

I sat down. She was never one of those people with whom you could argue, but rather she commanded you and you found yourself doing her bidding.

She said, 'Just now when they called me down here you took the message for me on the telephone. Have you any memory of why it was they wanted me?'

Of course I had. The whole thing had happened but a few minutes ago and was quite fresh in my memory. 'It was a case that had just been brought in. They said that it was an accident.'

'Yes,' she repeated slowly, 'that was it; it was a street accident,' and I saw her looking at me with that meaning look as though she would convey something to me. I was strung up. I had just been through that frightful scene with Flower, and the only person I could think of was Ray. Surely she was not trying to tell me that he had had an accident in his car?

'Ray?' I said at last. 'You don't mean . . .'

She shook her head.

'No, Dr. Harper has not been hurt; he is on his way to us now. You see, it was his wife.'

I might have known as much.

'She must have dashed out of the house in that crazy temper of hers, and then rushed straight into the road without looking what was coming. It is so unthinkable that anyone should ever allow themselves to get into such an awful mental state.'

I felt my lips going dry, and I stared at Miss Vaughan as though it were through a haze. The strange thing was that everything in the room seemed to go misty, everything save her eyes, which were staring at me, and her reassuring voice, doing its best to calm me.

'She isn't very seriously hurt?'

'It is rather difficult to tell, and the doctors are with her now. Luckily Dr. Clements was just coming down the stairs on his way from a patient here. She is quite unconscious, and he said something about her skull being fractured.'

I thought instantly of what that meant, and was horrified.

'Will they operate?'

'No one can say yet. They are examining her now. We have got to wait and be patient.'

It seemed dreadful to be waiting here for the verdict. Although she had been so jealous of me, and had flung herself into such a rage this morning, I did not wish her any ill. It is a terrible thing to wish anybody dead, and I knew directly Miss Vaughan mentioned her fractured skull that it might mean death.

I said, 'Please, Miss Vaughan, don't think that I wish her any ill. It is a terrible thing to have happened, and something must be done to save her life. Something *must* be done.'

She said very simply and earnestly, and it only verified all my previous knowledge of her:

'We can do nothing more. There are some things which rest in the hands of Providence, and we can only have faith in that Providence and know that everything is ordained for the best.'

I wish that words were not such futile and empty things.

I find myself in difficulties and trying to put what I felt into sentences, trying to express myself, for there is so much that I want to say. I waited there and listened to the sounds of the doctors coming down the stairs, and somebody said that Ray was there. I wanted to go to him, to stand by him and help him in any way that I could, but I was torn two ways. You see, I felt myself to be in the light of 'the other woman,' and it is not a happy position in which to find yourself.

I could not thrust myself forward and attend to Flower, for whom I would have done anything in the world that could be done. This is the truth. Yet I knew that if she became conscious I should be the very last person who ought to attend her.

'No, you must wait here,' Miss Vaughan insisted. 'It is perhaps the hardest thing for you to do, but you must wait.'

It *was* the hardest thing to do.

She went out to see what was happening, and she seemed to be gone for an eternity. I felt, left to myself like that, I should go mad. My whole world was in a state of upheaval. I might never see him again, I might never see her again. And during this time it wasn't our two selves that I thought most of, but of her. I wanted her to get well more than I had ever wanted anything; it seemed incredible.

Hours passed; probably they were only

minutes, but they seemed to be dragging because I was so distraught. Then Miss Vaughan came back.

'They are not operating.'

'Not?'

'No. There would be no chance, and she would only die on the table. I am afraid it is a terrible head wound. She will not recover consciousness and, thank Heaven, she will not suffer any pain. I don't think she had any knowledge of what happened; it was all too quick for that.'

She turned to me, and I saw that her face was genuinely distressed. Her eyes were full of tears.

'Perhaps I am silly, and perhaps I am taking it too much to heart, but it seems to me so dreadful that anybody should go out that way. It seems to be all wrong, and I am dreadfully sorry for her.'

I said, 'I am terribly sorry too,' and then suddenly I did something which is very rare for me. I think that I had been through too much and could not go on any longer. The tension snapped. The room spun round me and I felt everything going black in gyrating spots. I felt the darkness rising up from the floor and engulfing me.

I fainted.

# 9

I find it very difficult to write of what happened in between. I only know that it seemed that I lay in darkness for a long while, and that when I recovered I was in bed in one of the rooms right at the top of the home, the cheap little rooms where only the poorest patients are put.

I did not know what lay ahead. Somehow I felt that I did not want to see Ray again, not after a dreadful thing like this; not until we had found our normal selves and had recovered our balance. I did not want to go to Malta.

I was going to be ill.

I realized that all these incidents of the past few months had been leading up to the crisis which had come now, and that I must have crocked up. I lay there in a sort of dim twilight, and when Miss Vaughan came to see me I could not even ask her about Flower. I don't think I wanted to know. They sent Tenny up to me, to see if she could stir me, but even poor old Tenny could not wake me out of that horrid state of lethargy.

I can't write about it.

I lay there and I felt too ill to worry any more. I did not care if I ever got up again. I did not care if I lay here for an eternity; life seemed to have been so unfair to me and so hard, and I just believed that I had not got the strength left to face the future.

Then one day the door opened and I saw Ray

standing there.

He shut the door behind him and came quietly across the floor to the side of my bed, and stood looking down at me, as I had so often seen him standing beside patients. His eyes were full of sympathy.

He said, 'This won't do, you know,' and again it was a remark I had heard him make to other people when they lay as I did.

'I know,' I admitted.

'You have got to get better, you have got to rouse yourself. Like this you will just fret away, and there is nothing for you to fret yourself about.'

I lay there staring up at him, and he began to talk. He treated me like a child, like someone who does not quite understand what has been happening, and has to be told the string of events to be brought into contact with the affairs of to-day.

'It was a silly thing to go down like you did,' he said, 'just when the whole world was changing. Miss Vaughan told me about you; she told me about the scene before that, the scene which made poor Flower rush off in that crazy way she did. She never saw the car coming, and I believe even if she had seen it she would not have cared. When she got one of those attacks she was quite uncontrollable.'

I still could not speak. I knew then that I wanted to know how she was, but I had only to lie still and he would tell me.

'Thank God she never suffered!' he said, and his voice was low. 'Thank God she went out without a flutter of pain; she just ceased to be. She was making us so very unhappy, and herself, too. She had never been a happy person, poor little soul. She never could have been. That's all over—a closed chapter, something that has slipped into the past and has become part of that past. The future is ours.'

'I know,' I said. No more.

'You are not going to Malta, Dallas; you are staying here in London, here, with me. We have suffered so much, my dear, we can't go on this way. I am going to get a licence and arrange for the marriage at once.'

'Our marriage?'

'Yes, Dallas, our marriage. What is the object in waiting? What is the point in staying a single day longer? We love one another, my sweet, and that is sufficient justification for marriage.'

'But Flower?'

He shook his head. 'If Flower had lived catastrophe was bound to overtake us. I'm glad in a way, though not that she should have gone out like that. There was tragedy ahead for all of us; we knew it. Perhaps death was the kindest and the swiftest way. Let us forget and start living our own lives at last.'

I put out my hands, and then I knew that he had lifted me up into his arms, and that he was kissing me with all the tenderness of a man who has kissed you in imagination so many times, and has only just come into his rightful heritage.

I cannot tell you any more about it, because the rest is so lovely that it becomes almost sacred. It is so beautiful that there are no words fair enough with which to describe it.

We are amazingly happy.

We are not two, but one. I adore him, and I think that he worships the very ground on which I walk.

Life does not seem to be long enough to contain so much that is exquisite. They say that truth is stranger than fiction, and I, looking back into my own life, and reading my own story, think so, too.

We met in that nursing home, in the actual theatre. We met and we loved. We very nearly lost one another, and yet we married. Now I am his for always. I have my dreams. I am a lucky woman.

'Whenever I look at you, Dallas,' Miss Vaughan says, 'I always feel that it is a case of love finding the way.'

Perhaps she is right.



Photoset, printed and bound in Great Britain by
REDWOOD BURN LIMITED, Trowbridge, Wiltshire